STOCKHOLM

SEBASTYEN DUGAS

1

Jimmy Carrera was circling in his apartment in the Villeray neighbourhood. He couldn't stand to wait any longer. Every day around 5:00 pm, it was like hell. The endless minutes remaining to see actress Laura Labelle on-screen and discovering the fate awaiting her was unbearable. He recorded each of the episodes and analyzed them in depth afterwards. He dissected every word, every movement of the protagonists of the TV show "Madeleine's Crazy Adventure." Analyzing Laura's facial expressions, those of her game partners. He wanted to decipher the subtle messages, the secret messages.

He thought it was ridiculous to fall in love with an actress because of the role she was playing in fiction, but it was involuntary: he had a crush on her. She disturbed him so much that he was intimidated to see her on-screen or on a picture. He didn't talk about his love for her with anyone for fear of being ridiculed, even though several people had discovered that he was smitten by her.

Everything was fine until Jimmy detected very subtle signs that convinced him that the young actress was in danger. All the elements Jimmy had analyzed were crystal clear. He could read the subtext: someone was trying to eliminate Laura, to humiliate her.

Jimmy looked at the wall lined with pictures and articles about Laura on his left. She was beautiful.

He knew everything about her and her role as Martine. He had kept all the articles, interviews, everything he could find about her. He consulted the beautiful actress's Instagram and Facebook accounts several times a day.

He had tried to establish ties with her, but had not been successful. But that was normal—lots of fans were trying to get close to her because she was so popular. She couldn't answer everyone. He had received some terse responses from her, but he was convinced that they had been written by the team that managed her social media accounts.

The important thing was the love he had for her. His obsession meant he knew her from top to bottom, as you would a sister, a brother, or a lover.

From the start, Jimmy had been content to look at her from a distance, refusing to interfere with her life, staying away. Except this time, it was different. He still didn't want to meddle with her life—he didn't want to look like a freak—but he couldn't let things go, sitting there with his arms crossed while she was in tremendous danger. And it certainly wasn't that idiot François Béliveau, his alleged lover, who was going to take care of her. François was far too full of himself, far too busy taking stupid selfies and polluting his Instagram account.

Jimmy had to take charge. But how? No one would believe him. It was one thing for the character played by Laura to die in the show. But it was something else for her to suffer the same thing in real life.

Not under his watch.

Jimmy admitted that the actress's death ploy was well planned. No one could have predicted that such a thing would happen. At least, no one who wasn't paying attention. No one had been as methodical as him in analyzing the clues and discovering the plot; no one had put in as much effort as he had.

Jimmy had asked Laura to chat with him privately on Facebook, but there was no answer. He had no choice but to communicate directly with her agent.

The show started while Jimmy was biting his nails, worried sick. He screamed in rage when Martine's character stumbled as she dropped the tray full of wine glasses she was carrying, while the crowd laughed. They wanted to humiliate her, and everyone was an accomplice. Laura's face twisted with shame. How could they do this to her? What had she done to them to be treated so cruelly?

Jimmy had assessed all the possibilities: contacting the police, confronting the producers of the show, notifying his agent, her famous friends, but he didn't do anything about it. He feared that alerting her loved ones would speed up the attack on Laura, or make him look like a madman. They would never understand the logic behind Jimmy's conclusion that Laura was at risk. It would take too long to explain, and he didn't have time to waste.

He thought of going to the TV studio, but the broadcasts were not live, and he didn't know the filming schedules. Time was running out, especially since they were probably close to shooting the fateful scene. He had to act now.

He decided to act the next day. The situation was critical. His brother Dominic had challenged him to do something about it. Dominic was the only one who believed him, and he had encouraged him to follow through with his plan.

Jimmy headed to his bedroom and looked at his reflection in the mirror over his mahogany desk. His features looked drawn, the stress having deepened wrinkles on his forehead. He was only 25 years old but looked ten years older. His black hair was messy, and he hadn't showered for at least 72 hours. He was not sleeping, consumed by the anxiety of what was going on. He had made at least fifty different plans without finding a suitable one. But right now, he resolved that he would shower, put on clean clothes and be presentable so as not to frighten her. She didn't know him; she wasn't going to trust him just like that simply because he wanted to protect her. The old maxim repeated itself in his head: "We only have one chance to make an excellent first impression." It all started from there.

"She's attracted to blue-eyed blonds," Dominic said to him from the hallway.

"I know all this very well." Jimmy was disgusted by what he saw in the mirror. His reflection showed the black of his hair and the brown of his eyes back to him.

He had bought the dye earlier at the pharmacy, and had coloured his hair that evening. But there was nothing to be done about his brown eyes: he was unable to wear contact lenses. He couldn't stand to put his fingers in his eyes.

He analyzed his silhouette in the mirror for several seconds and was disappointed with the protrusion of his stomach. He didn't take care of himself. A woman like Laura was used to dating supermodels, like those found in magazines. Jimmy had only a limp and a disappointing body to offer. He was going to have to wear loose-fitting clothes to hide his disadvantageous looks. Dominic had kept telling him to get in shape, but he didn't have the energy. His brother's disgusted looks did nothing to help his self-esteem.

He showered and rethought his plan several times, talking to himself as if he was talking to Laura. The echo of the shower amplified his voice.

He took two melatonin pills, hoping to get a good night's rest.

⁓

EXHAUSTED, Laura Labelle was lying on the couch of her chic apartment on Plateau Mont-Royal in Montreal. She had worked hard in recent years. Although many people had warned her about the load of working in a daily TV show, she had underestimated the impact of the long days of filming on her body and her mind.

She had no energy left.

The end of her relationship with François Béliveau had been challenging. The inevitable breakup had gathered speed when she developed a crush on a cute cameraman she'd met on a late-night talk show. She was not in love with Béliveau; she never had been. The relationship had been instigated by her former agent, who thought it would be beneficial for their respective careers to be in a power couple. She had tolerated the situation until she'd fallen in love with Bruno Morency, a young man three years older than her. She thought he was very mature, at least compared to Béliveau's frivolous and immature teenage temperament.

Her agent didn't approve of her relationship with Morency. For him, the cameraman was a nobody who could only damage her brand. Laura had met Bruno a few weeks before she'd told François Béliveau that their relationship was over. Béliveau had not taken it so well, not at all. He had always taken her for granted, believing that she would never dare to question their arrangement.

But when he felt he was losing control of the situation, Béliveau had suddenly become kind and caring.

Too little, too late.

Anyway, Laura only had eyes for Bruno. When she broke up with Béliveau, she knew that she was leaving behind her status as half of a prominent couple, which had brought them both enormous visibility and generous contracts.

Clearly, her new boyfriend would not attract the same interest from sponsors, but she didn't care. Her love for Bruno was more important than anything else. She had never known anyone like him before. She had never felt such an attraction for a man in her life.

It was not only the infernal rhythm of the shooting of the TV show that exhausted her, but also the promotional activities to which she had to submit herself contractually. All these public appearances, all these interactions with the fans, represented a tremendous strain for her, due in large part to her introverted nature. She would far more prefer to spend the evenings in her pyjamas, watching TV series and movies, wrapped up in a blanket and snuggled up against her lover.

She couldn't imagine why people would want to be famous at all costs. For her, fame was the dark side of her job. If there were a way that she could make a living as an actress while remaining anonymous, she would be willing to pay a lot of money for it.

Given her agent's opinion of her life choices and her new lover, Laura had decided to fire him and have her affairs handled by Mike Tougas, another prominent agent in the industry who had been highly recommended to her by a colleague. She had told Laura how understanding and humane Tougas was and that he did not put any undue pressure on his clients. His role was to advise them as best he could, but the final choice was up to the artist, even if it was against what he was advocating.

His mantra was that the agent was working for the client and not the other way around. Laura had appreciated the few meetings she had had with him, but it was mainly her immediate complicity with Anouk, Tougas's wife, that convinced her. She was a sublime woman who immediately put you at ease with her warm smile and big, comforting green eyes.

Even though she hadn't yet discussed the subject with Mike, Laura wanted it to be clear that her relationship with Bruno was paramount to her, that it was non-negotiable. She wouldn't hide him. He would be at her side in public outings, and it would be evident to everyone that he was her lover. She didn't care if it offended some of her fans; that would be their problem. She would tell him all of this soon; the four had agreed to share a meal, to establish their expectations of how things should go and to seal the deal.

Tomorrow, Laura would attend a signing session with another actress from the TV show. The simple thought of facing a horde of admirers made her shiver. She had wracked her brains for a way to avoid being present but had found no sufficiently credible reason that would not be a breach of contract.

It was getting late. Bruno was working, but he'd join her in bed after he got home. Already in a bathrobe, Laura was wearing her big moose-head slippers that her mother had bought her a few years ago. She smiled as she remembered the moment she had opened the Christmas gift under her mother's mocking eye. Mme. Labelle knew very well that her cute little girl was not fond of this kind of attire.

But over time, Laura had come to appreciate these big slippers. They were indeed comfortable, but it was above all the memory of that crazy laugh shared with her mother that gave them such a special cachet. She had only her mother left; her beloved father had died suddenly of a heart attack when she was 13 years old. She had wondered a few times whether her failed relationships with men were not related to the lack of a fatherly presence at a crucial time of her development. With that said, she was convinced that Bruno was different, that he was the right one, and that it was going to work.

"Dad would have loved him," she thought melancholically.

The memory of how they'd fallen in love at first sight was still vivid in her mind. As one of the guests of a popular late-night talk show, she had scanned the crowd with her eyes during a commercial break as she always did, and had encountered the intense look of a cameraman she'd never seen before.

Unlike other men, most of whom were intimidated by her, the cameraman had maintained his gaze with such insistence that Laura's heart had begun racing. She had never felt this before, such magnetism at first sight. She didn't know how to handle all this, but one thing was for sure: this man had a strong power over her.

The cameraman had put his face back into his camera when the signal came back on the air, but she kept looking at him until she realized that the host had asked her a question she hadn't understood, still immersed in her new fantasy. She had come out of her stupor after a few seconds and asked the host to repeat the question, blushing like a little girl caught red-handed by her parents. She had recovered her composure, and the rest of the evening had gone smoothly.

Laura had glanced furtively at the cameraman once or twice after that, but he had paid only brief attention to her between breaks. The long, languid gazes had given way to short, discreet glances.

At the end of the program, the host had invited the team and guests who wished to join him for a meal in a nearby restaurant. Laura had agreed to go there in the hope that the handsome cameraman would also be there. She had been happy to see that this was true and had sat across the table from him. They had not talked much, just giving themselves more and more intense looks as time went by. The young man's cheerful smile, the brightness in his eyes... Laura had the impression that he was reading his soul. They had agreed to meet again alone a few days later in a Montreal bar.

Laura had a gift for knowing whether a man was interested in her or not. This guy, Bruno—it was apparent he was completely gaga for her; she could swear it.

And of course, the feeling was mutual. Laura wanted to

explore that chemistry they had felt for each other, see where it would lead them.

The evening had gone very well. Bruno had a very good sense of humour, and he was very endearing and reassuring. Laura had detected no signs of mental flaws, no suspicious reactions, no prolonged silence. Everything had flowed perfectly.

She thought it was too good to be true, but she didn't care. She was embarking on this adventure without restraint. Either she would fall madly in love with this guy, and it would be the beginning of a beautiful story, or she would run straight into a wall and get rejected. It wouldn't be the first time. It was okay; she knew how to reconstruct herself.

As they left the bar, discussing a trivial matter that she had already forgotten, Bruno had grabbed her by the waist and pulled her towards him, then glued his soft lips firmly against hers.

Laura felt like her legs had been sawn off. Luckily Bruno was holding her firmly. She closed her eyes, dazed by the intoxicating dance of her surroundings revolving around her. They had kissed for a few seconds, but it seemed like an eternity to her. Not because it bothered her. On the contrary. She didn't want it to stop.

It was so good; it was so beautiful.

On her way home, alone in her car, she had a blissful smile on her face. For a rare time in her life, she allowed herself to be happy without wondering what would go wrong to counterbalance her joy.

Then, a car coming in the opposite direction on Jacques-Cartier Bridge had crashed into the guardrail, causing frightening fire sparks to spill out. The vehicle had then zigzagged dangerously towards Laura's car. She had been terrified, sure that they would collide; it was inevitable. The moment of exaltation she had experienced a few seconds earlier would evaporate and plunge her back into the depressing reality in which she had been wallowing for so long. Nothing good could happen to her without being followed by something terrible. A friend had once told her that she was nurturing an unhappiness gene. That if she had a positive attitude, she'd attract good things. Laura had rejected this esoteric theory out of hand; she didn't believe in that nonsense.

The other car's headlights blinded her; it was a matter of milliseconds before the two cars struck each other.

For some reason, the images of her kiss with Bruno came back to her mind as clearly as if she was still living it, and suddenly she believed that no matter what happened, nothing would darken that magical moment she had experienced. Not even a dazzling collision with that out-of-control car. No one could take away the plenitude she'd felt when she thought about the kiss.

She closed her eyes, ready to face what life was going to throw at her.

Then, just like that, the car had veered away at the last moment, barely avoiding Laura's vehicle. She had sighed with relief as she continued on her way.

When she told her positive-thinking friend about what happened, he had smiled in satisfaction and told her that she could not have had a better proof of the power of the mind. Laura didn't know if he was right or if it was just a coincidence, but she had played along. Maybe he was right after all. He looked so happy all the time, while even though she had everything a person could hope for, she was the saddest person she knew.

The next day, another task awaited her; she had to break up with François Béliveau. The relationship had been over for a long time, but she hadn't been willing to admit it. Mostly because of the pressure from her former agent and everything she was likely to lose. She did the deed a few hours after she got up, driven by a sudden urge to put an end to all this. That was another proof that she should plunge right into her relationship with Bruno.

Bruno was so charming, so well-rounded. Always in a good mood, he never got angry. In fact, the only time she had seen him out of control was during an argument with his ex-agent. He had told Bruno—or rather, ordered him—to stay away from Laura in public. The fans had to believe she hadn't left François Béliveau to throw herself into another man's arms right away.

He said that she had to live through her heartbreak, even if it was only smoke and mirrors to preserve her brand image.

Secretly, the agent wanted Laura to grow tired of Bruno and return to her senses. Being in a relationship with a "civilian," as artists call people who are not from their field, would be damaging to her image.

Bruno did not appreciate the agent's tone and told him so. Even though Laura felt uneasy seeing the two men fighting, she was charmed by her lover's character and how he didn't let himself get trampled on, by the way he cherished their relationship. At the end of this thunderous argument, Bruno had left and slammed the door behind him. Laura had told her agent that if he didn't accept her new relationship, she would fire him. The agent had tried to reason with her by being less than complimentary about Bruno, a miserable freelancer who had no money, no clout, and no potential for the future. A man who would take advantage of her and her wealth. He guaranteed her that her fans would never understand that she had left a man of François Béliveau's calibre for this loser.

It was too much, and she had fired him on the spot and left to chase after her boyfriend. As she walked out the door, she heard the agent scream that she was a stupid little bitch, that she was going to lose everything, but she ignored him and kept running.

She had given enough attention to that jerk.

She was hoping Mike Tougas had more judgment. Because it was clear to her: no one would get between Bruno and her.

No one.

She turned off the television. She wanted to wait for Bruno to return, but he wouldn't be here for two more hours, and she was falling asleep. He had his key anyway, so he could let himself in and join her later.

After a quick shower, she went to bed and quickly sank into a deep sleep.

2

"Wake up, lazy head. It'll be a great day today. The world belongs to those who get up early."

Jimmy opened his eyes and looked at the clock.

5:15 in the morning.

"For God's sake, Dominic, let me sleep."

"No, wake up. Come on."

Jimmy saw his brother's shadow leave his room, and he got up, growling.

Dominic could be such a pain in the ass.

Jimmy looked again at his reflection in the mirror to contemplate his thick, now blonde hair. He was disappointed to realize that the colour did not look natural. There was nothing he could do about it now; he didn't have time for this.

Out of the corner of his eye, he saw a shadow passing behind him. He jumped as he stared at the shape but saw nothing other than the white wall at the other end of the room. His heart went crazy, and he took two deep breaths to calm down and lower his pulse.

"Dom?"

His brother didn't answer.

A quick look at his front door confirmed that both latches were locked. The patio door was also closed. Besides, it creaked so much that even if someone were to try to sneak in, it would be impossible. He took one last deep breath and headed for the living room, where he found his brother staring out the window.

"Why didn't you answer me?"

Dominic looked at him dubiously. Jimmy dropped it; he probably hadn't heard him. He felt a mixture of adrenalin and excitement as he realized that this was the day he would finally talk to Laura.

He was nervous and anxious. Calm down, he told himself. If he weren't in control of his emotions when talking to her, she'd freak out. What he would tell her was not easy to understand, and he had to be cool and in control.

He turned on his laptop to look up Laura's agent's phone number and dialled it on his cell phone.

The person answering told him that the firm no longer represented Laura Labelle. Astonished, Jimmy asked her the name of the new agent, but the woman had already hung up. He cursed her for endangering Laura's life through her inaction.

He began to search the internet and landed on a gossip site that said that Mike Tougas' agency now represented Laura. He didn't know if this was right or if it was mere gossip, but he had nothing to lose.

Before calling the agency, Jimmy looked at a photograph of Laura that he particularly liked. He took a few seconds to admire it. Laura was sitting with her legs crossed, her left leg raised to support both arms. Her long, black hair was tucked back, showing off the right side of her face. Her full lips outlined a perfectly symmetrical smile and showed a set of magnificent, unnaturally white teeth.

Laura's eyes were expressive, as usual, and Jimmy once again felt a strong connection with her.

She was gorgeous—not too big, not too thin. Not too tall, not too small. "Absolutely perfect," he thought.

He was swooning over the photo like an artist admiring his work.

After being taken out of his thoughts by a truck passing by, he noticed Dominic staring at him impassively. Jimmy smiled at him and called the agency number.

"Tougas and Gosselin Agency."

Jimmy sat up in his chair as if it gave him more credibility. "Hi, I'd like to speak with Mike Tougas, please."

"Mr. Tougas is not here. May I take a message?"

Jimmy fumed. He didn't have time to wait for Tougas to bother to call him back, God knew when. This was urgent.

"Maybe you can help me. I'm looking to talk to Laura Labelle. I understand that your agency now represents her. I need to talk to her urgently. Could you give me her cell phone number or a number where I can reach her?"

"Sir, we never give out that kind of information, come on. I'm going to ask Mr. Tougas to—"

"I know, ma'am," Jimmy said, interrupting her, "but it's a matter of life or death—do you understand? We don't have time to worry about protocol. I want to talk to her about the demise of her character in the show and what it means to her."

There was a moment of silence.

"The death of her character? I think you're mistaken, sir. On the contrary, Mr. Tougas is negotiating the extension of Laura's contract. Believe me, no one intends to make such a central and popular character disappear from the show."

Jimmy was surprised by this news, but concluded that the producers of the series were using this scheme to ensure

Laura's presence when they planned to kill her both on the show and in the real world. They were going to fake an accident and then pocket the proceeds from all the events that would pay tribute to Laura, from DVD sales. And of course, her death would provide a much-needed boost for a TV series that was losing momentum. These men were only thinking about their wallets, Jimmy knew. The hell with it if anyone should suffer from it in the process. They were collateral damage.

"Look, I know things you don't know," Jimmy said. "I know that her character is going to die and that she faces a great danger of suffering the same fate. I beg you to give me her phone number or Mike Tougas' home number."

"As I told you, I'm not authorized to give you the personal contact numbers of our artists and employees. Have a good day, sir."

She hung up despite Jimmy's pleas. He threw his cell phone on the couch in front of him.

"You stupid bitch," he said to himself. "She must be in on it too."

He paced in circles around his apartment, simmering with rage. After a few minutes of ruminating about what he was going to do, he reopened his laptop and ran a search on Laura Labelle. He had to find a way to reach her.

Then, on a social media site, he saw an ad mentioning that actors from the show would be in the area that night for a signing session. It would take place in a shopping mall near his home. He thought it was a sign of fate. What were the chances of that happening?

The autograph session was to take place at Galeries St-Hubert at 4:00 p.m. It was perfect; it gave him about six hours to refine his game plan. Considering that he had thought he would only talk to Laura on the phone, this was an unexpected windfall. He would meet with her face-to-face! Another indication from destiny that he was doing the right thing. The universe was sending him unequivocal signals. Things were setting themselves up.

He had previously attended events where Laura was present, but he had never found the courage to talk to her, content to watch her from a distance. She was so warm with people, so kind. It had made him fall even more in love with her.

He had sent her lots of messages via social media, telling her how beautiful he thought she was in a scene or how the dress she had worn on a red carpet had suited her well. He had even taken the liberty of giving her advice on her craft, on her life. He had told her how much he disapproved of her relationship with François Béliveau,

She had sometimes replied to him, but Jimmy wasn't sure if it was her responding or just her social media crew.

This time, he knew, he would have to overcome his shyness and talk to her. He thought back to that picture of her he had been contemplating, and suddenly he felt afraid of being paralyzed by her bewitching gaze. If he were intimidated by her stare from an innocent photo, it would be worse in person.

"Pull yourself together, Jimmy," Dominic said. "Laura Labelle is an ordinary person like you and me. All you have to do is think like that, and she won't intimidate you."

He was right. Jimmy would have to approach her like she was a long-time friend, ignoring the aura that surrounds people we idolize.

For the rest of the day, time passed very slowly. Jimmy, a newly unemployed worker, checked his digital watch constantly. He had to find a way to distract his mind until the fateful hour, or he would go mad. He asked his brother to play a board game, but he refused. Dominic never wanted to do anything. He just stayed there, looking at him and giving him advice.

Jimmy watched a re-run of a show he had already seen,

partly to adapt to Laura's expression and partly in hopes that it would relax him.

He poured himself a glass of cold water, and as he sat down, he saw Laura languorously kissing the man who was playing her lover in the show. Every time Laura kissed an actor, it was like a stab to Jimmy's chest, like when you catch the one you love with someone else. He shook himself. It was only a role, he reminded himself. Laura was an actress. Understandably, her character would kiss someone. There was nothing authentic about that. Nothing as real as the love Jimmy had for her.

Once he had calmed down, he became absorbed by the scene, imagining that it was him she was kissing with such passion.

Suddenly, Laura's eyes turned directly to the camera, towards Jimmy, as she carried on kissing the other guy.

Jimmy's heart went crazy. He didn't remember this scene, even though he had seen it dozens of times. Moreover, the actors never looked at the camera before. Laura was still kissing the other person, keeping Jimmy in sight, and then she sneered at him with a sly smile. Jimmy's heart began to pound with excitement. He turned to his brother, but he was not there.

Laura stopped kissing the actor and then sensually licked her partner's neck, still staring languorously at the camera. Jimmy looked away, no longer able to cope with all the sexual tension. He had never felt so disturbed in his entire life; he didn't know how to react.

After a few seconds, he looked at the screen again, but a shampoo commercial was playing. He was shocked that the scene had ended so abruptly and grabbed the TV remote control to rewind back to it. He stopped as Laura threw her arms around her fictional lover's neck and kissed him with passion. Jimmy waited for the scene to replay, but something was not right. This time, Laura kissed the actor for only a few seconds before leaving the room. The show then cut to the shampoo ad. Laura hadn't looked at the camera at all.

He replayed the scene several times, thinking he hadn't found the right location on the recording, but each time, it came back to the moment when Laura kissed the guy and then left the room.

Then, that damn shampoo commercial.

What was going on? He couldn't have imagined all this. He was furious with himself for looking away from the screen for a split second. Now, he was even more convinced that he would never be able to withstand Laura's intense look in person. He would be responsible for her death because he was too fragile.

"What's going on?" said his brother, who had just reappeared.

Jimmy reported what he had just seen, but Dominic laughed at him, saying he was hallucinating, confusing his fantasy with reality. He was probably right.

Jimmy noticed a strange glint in Dominic's eyes, as if a white flash of lightning had quickly passed through his pupils. Dominic asked him why he was looking at him like that, but Jimmy didn't answer. He was imagining things, he told himself. It was probably due to his fear about meeting with Laura.

To distract himself, Jimmy decided to walk down to the park a few blocks away from his home. He was not sure if he was imagining things, but it seemed passers-by were randomly looking at him. Was it because of his grotesque blond hair? Jimmy had a tendency to attribute intentions to people; this had caused him trouble in the past. It was also the main reason he didn't have many friends except for Dominic, his aunt, and his friend Mathieu.

He went on his way, avoiding people's eyes. He sat on a park bench and took several deep breaths, trying to regain his senses. He didn't have the luxury of screwing things up with Laura. Not under these circumstances. He wouldn't be able to live with himself if his mission failed; failure meant that she would die.

He hadn't been able to save the other women in his life; he was going to save this one.

Even if he died trying.

3

That afternoon, Laura Labelle made her way to the event in a taxi, wishing she hadn't accepted. Meeting her fans demanded more and more energy from her. As much as she had loved this part of her career at first, it annoyed her considerably now. She had never liked being the centre of attention before she was an actress. That was why her mother had been so surprised by her career choice. Her daughter, who preferred reading in her room rather than going to parties with her friends. Her daughter, who didn't want to go to her graduation because it meant being on stage. Her daughter, who was unable to sleep the night before an oral presentation in high school.

But Laura had explained to her mother that playing a role was not the same because she could hide behind her character. She could turn on the switch to play a part and then turn it off again. When Laura returned to being Laura, she regained her introverted nature, which detested crowds. It was difficult to explain; even Laura didn't know how she lived with this duality.

But that's the way it was; there was nothing more to add.

She shivered as the taxi took a right turn, and she saw the

shopping mall in the distance. Every fibre in her body urged her to flee, to ask the driver to do a U-turn. But she had duties. Mike Tougas was going to be there; her face was on the promotional posters. She had to go in there. She had no other choice. Feeling compelled to do what she hated brought tears to her eyes.

Fortunately, Bruno was going to meet her there at some point. Laura didn't know Mike Tougas very well, but she hoped he would acknowledge her love for Bruno and not attempt to control her private life. If she needed to change agents every week until she found one who would accept her relationship, she would. No one would ever impose anything on her again, not after the François Béliveau fiasco.

Never again.

She paid for her ride and walked along the brick wall of the building towards a secondary entrance door, trying to blend in as much as possible with her surroundings. As she entered, she spotted the team of technicians who were finishing installing the tables and, to her right, her colleague Martine, who waved at her. Laura breathed a sigh of relief; Martine was good company. The two of them got along very well.

Laura walked towards her, forcing a smile.

AFTER LEAVING the bookstore with the last John Grisham for his aunt's birthday, Jimmy walked around the aisles of the mall, avoiding wandering near where the signing session would take place in a few hours. He was wondering if Dominic was right after all. Perhaps the only way Laura would agree to follow him would be through coercion. At the end of the day, only the result counted. He quickly dismissed the idea. He didn't see how Laura would be responsive under these conditions, and, in any case, he had no means of forcing her to oblige. He didn't have a gun. The only weapon he had was at home. For a brief moment, he regretted not having brought it with him. If it turned out that he needed to use force, it would have been useful.

But no, nothing good happens with a gun when you're on edge, Jimmy thought, arguing with himself as though he had a devil and an angel in his head.

He wished he hadn't told Mathieu that he would be coming to the restaurant with Laura tonight. Mathieu had giggled with an expression suggesting that it was unlikely to happen.

Jimmy's idea was to convince Laura to join him at the restaurant, Deux Cigognes, where Mathieu was working. There, privately, he would explain to her that he was afraid for her and give her the results of his investigation.

He watched the technicians who were installing the tables and lighting equipment on the premises. There was no sign of Laura, and a worm of doubt began to gnaw at him. What if Laura had cancelled her appearance?

He panicked.

One of the technicians who noticed his arrival asked him if he could help him.

"Do you know if Laura Labelle will be here tonight?"

"Who?"

Jimmy couldn't conceive of anyone not knowing who Laura Labelle was. The man's colleague intervened.

"She's on the poster, so I guess she'll be here. What do you think?"

Jimmy didn't care for the technician's arrogant tone, but he disregarded it. He left without asking any further questions. People were so out of touch, he thought angrily. Imagine if something terrible happened to Laura, and these two morons did nothing to help the only person who was meant to save her. They'd look like complete idiots.

The waiting became unbearable for Jimmy, who didn't notice that Laura had entered by a different door.

Restless and uneasy, Jimmy went to sit in the food court to sip a soft drink and take some deep breaths. His nervousness worried him. He had to calm down somehow. A shadow passing in his peripheral vision made him startle, but just like the previous time at the apartment, there was nobody there. Then another shadow passed close to him, but this time to his right. Was he losing his mind? He was clearly agitated, but to imagine fictional shadows?

He got to his feet; he could no longer bear to wait until the fateful hour came when he would finally speak to Laura and warn her about the dangers she was in for.

He sat down again; he was also afraid to fail. How would he react if he was unable to convince Laura and make her see the light?

Would he just go back home with his tail between his legs? Unthinkable.

And Mathieu, with his fucking condescending look, would not fail to inquire where Laura was if Jimmy went alone to the restaurant.

No, he had to succeed at all costs.

He heard loud music from a distance and realized that the event had just begun. There was a massive crowd in the mall corridors now, and people were converging towards where the actors would soon appear. Jimmy looked at his watch; it was time. He took a deep breath and got up. After a few steps, his legs nearly buckled and he grabbed a table for support.

God, he'd never make it through. His inability to manage his emotions disheartened him. Dominic would never have this kind of problem. He was so in control of everything, so clear of mind and purpose. He wouldn't be impressed by a fucking actress. Dominic didn't care what anyone else thought. Jimmy had always envied him for that.

He wished Dominic could somehow infuse him with his strength, maybe telepathically. He needed it so much right now. Jimmy had asked his brother to come with him, but, as usual, he had refused without an explanation. Dominic never justified himself. If you pushed him too hard, he would become angry and sometimes even violent. Might as well not insist.

Jimmy moved slowly, trying to maintain his balance as a crowd of young people ran by him, laughing and talking so loudly that it hurt his eardrums. People could be unbearable sometimes. Crowds made him angry. But for now, all he cared about was getting to his destination on both feet.

He saw his reflection as he walked past a shop window. As always, he was disappointed with what he saw. His blond hair looked greenish; his blunt-shaped body was not sufficiently hidden under his loose-fitting clothes. Laura wouldn't want to have anything to do with him. His heart was racing so hard in his chest that he thought he was about to pass out. He stopped for a few seconds and took three deep breaths. He was sweating profusely. He was a mess. He turned to his left and staggered into a public men's room, where he bent over the sink and splashed his face with cold water. He looked in the mirror.

"Get your shit together, Jimmy, for crying out loud. You'll fail again. How many will you have to lose before you do something?"

He lowered his head. His nose was tingling like he was about to cry. He straightened up, sniffled, and walked to one of the free toilet cubicles. He closed the door behind him, locked it, and sat down. He wasn't going to get out of there until he felt ready. It was no use seeing Laura in this state of mind. He didn't know how he would manage to do it, but he had to find a way. He had only rarely done so since his mother's death, but now he closed his eyes and implored her to provide him with the necessary strength to save Laura.

Finally, he settled down and felt he was ready. As he opened his eyes, his focus was drawn by a shadow under the cubicle door. He held his breath for a few moments, but the shadow remained there. Like someone was standing in front of his booth.

But the shape was not human.

"What do you want from me?"

No answer. The shadow did not move.

"Hello?"

Nothing.

Irritated, Jimmy got up and banged on the door.

"Answer me! What do you want from me?"

A hesitant voice that he failed to recognize replied after a few seconds.

"Who are you talking to?"

"To you."

"I don't want anything. I just got here, man, I just want to wash my hands. Are you all right?"

The shadow had disappeared. Jimmy sat down again. He was going crazy. What was it with those damn shadows appearing and disappearing for no reason?

He waited until the men's room was empty before he opened the cubicle door and stepped out.

Strangely enough, all this had made him forget Laura, and he felt much better. A little stronger. A little more himself.

That was better than nothing.

"Hello, Laura. You look gorgeous."

Mike Tougas had just made his entrance, with all the commotion that characterized him. Laura smiled politely and accepted his embrace. The agent left her to greet his other clients, while Anouk stayed next to her.

"You seem worried," she said.

Laura was upset that she couldn't better hide her feelings. Anouk had immediately noticed that something was not right.

"Actually, I don't like this sort of stuff," Laura said. "I won't deny that I would rather have stayed home and watched movies."

Unexpectedly, Anouk didn't attempt to persuade her that everything was going to be all right. She simply smiled and told her that she understood. She also preferred to stay home, in her pyjamas, doing nothing.

Laura didn't know why, but this helped her relax a little. Perhaps simply expressing her uneasiness about the event had helped her calm down. And Anouk's confiding that she shared her reluctance also took a burden off her shoulders.

"Will Bruno be here tonight?" Anouk asked.

"Yes, but a little later."

The latest developments had occurred so quickly that Laura had not yet been able to discuss the details of her relationship with her new agent. She had fired the other one so fast that it looked like a spoiled child's spur-of-the-moment impulse. In any case, that was what her former agent was telling everyone who would listen. But for Laura, it had been far from an emotional decision. Quite the opposite; it had been long over-due. Laura needed an agent, not a stepmother who would meddle with her love life. The dinner planned for tonight was timely.

"It's time," said the event organizer, someone Laura had never seen before. Thundering music had been playing for a few minutes and Laura concluded that there would be an offi-cial presentation of Martine and herself, to her great dismay. She gnashed her teeth when she heard the overexcited voice of the host and the clamour of the many fans who had crammed into the area to meet them.

She had to put a smile on her face, to pretend she wanted to be there. The last thing Laura wanted was to read on social media that she'd looked like she wanted to be anywhere else. After all, it was thanks to her fans that she had such a great career; she owed them that much. She recalled the last encounters with her fans and calmed down, realizing that these people loved her and that, after all, it always went well—except for a few excited people here and there who were quickly ushered out.

"And now, in the role of Véronique Lagacé, may I introduce to you the magnificent Laura Labelle."

It was probably just a figment of her imagination, but she sensed that the cheers were more robust for her than they had been for Martine. This made her smile.

She was temporarily blinded by the spotlights, but she was able to reach her place, where she stood and cheerfully greeted the crowd before taking her seat.

"It's crowded," Martine said.

"Yeah, this is crazy."

"We're going to be all over Instagram tomorrow morning."

They both laughed. In the world of social media, you couldn't just sign a poster or a book. You also had to take a selfie with each fan. And each of these fans would then post their pictures on Twitter, on Facebook, and especially on Instagram.

The first fan to approach the table was a young man with brown hair and round glasses. Laura thought he looked like Harry Potter. He had a cute face and was probably about 12 years old.

"What is your name?" Laura said, with a pen in her hand.

"Samuel. I love you so much, you know. I think you're very pretty."

The young man's face turned scarlet, and Laura smiled tenderly at him.

"Oh, that's very sweet of you."

She wrote "To Samuel with affection, Laura." The young

man turned around and brandished his portable camera in front of him to take a picture of the two of them. Laura played along and smiled, trying to be convincing enough. Samuel looked at the picture and then thanked Laura, with sparkling eyes and a smile that went right up to his ears, and then left at full speed.

"Bruno has competition," Martine told her with a laugh.

"Yeah, right? Wasn't he cute? He was a sweetheart."

Laura had such an affection for children. Everyone told her she would make an amazing mother. While she had a lot of doubts about herself, she knew without reservation that she had maternal instincts. She'd make a great mom, no question about it. She'd had the best example from both her parents. They had been caring and very supportive. They had instilled good values in her and loved her unconditionally. Laura believed that this was the way you should love others, and this had burned her often when she first started dating. Men did not love her the same way in return. At least, according to her assessment.

She felt heavy-hearted when she remembered her father. She still could see him lying on the floor; he had fallen suddenly as he'd walked past her in the living room of the family house. The awful sound of her father's body crashing against the floor still echoed in her ears. She was 13 years old; she had understood right away that this was serious. He was 51 years old and had suffered a devastating heart attack that had given him no chance.

She shook herself inwardly and looked up to welcome the woman standing in front of her, smiling brightly.

"I love you so much in your role as Veronica," said the woman in a soft voice. "But beware of Julien, because he's not sincere. I don't trust him."

Laura put on a serious expression. "Okay, I guess you're right. I'll be careful."

She smiled at the woman and asked her name. It entertained her a great deal when people mixed up fiction with reality. It was often harmless, as with this woman, but sometimes it was more dramatic: occasionally, people became intrusive and aggressive, especially towards actors who played unsympathetic characters.

One of her colleagues had been approached in a grocery store by a sad individual who had said he wanted to take care of him—and not in a good way. Another had received several death threats when her character killed her child by drowning him in a bath during an episode.

Regardless of the statistics showing that Montreal was safer than ever, Laura felt that people were increasingly insane.

Robotically, she continued signing the posters that were presented to her. Later, she had no idea how many in total she had signed.

She smiled convincingly at people, interacting with them admirably well for someone who wanted to be elsewhere. It was like being outside her body, watching herself experience a moment she had no consciousness of. It was unreal, but at the same time, it showed how professional she had become. She did everything mechanically, without thinking. She could spend hours like this, in a secondary state, interacting with people. Every time she looked at the comments the next day on social media, Laura read that she was friendly and warm, that it was apparent that she loved her fans.

"One day, we will send robots instead of us to attend activities we are not interested in," she thought to herself. She would never see that in her lifetime, but she was sure it was unavoidable. Artificial intelligence was a field she was passionate about. She had been reading a lot about it. The possibilities were unimaginable and, at times, frightening.

The next person who stepped up was a strange-looking young man. He had coloured his hair with cheap dye and wore clothes that were too large for him. His hands were shaking, and he had troubled but gentle brown eyes. Laura asked what his name was.

"J... Jimmy."

It made her uncomfortable when people were overly intimidated by her. She signed the poster and smiled for the picture. As the man faced the other way to take the photo, Laura noticed his sweaty neck. Poor guy, she thought. He looked so nervous.

He turned and looked back at her, but instead of leaving, he stared at her without a word. She smiled to indicate to him that they were finished, but he leaned towards her and muttered something that she didn't understand.

"Excuse me?"

"Y—you're in....danger of dying, Laura. Come with me. I'll explain."

Instinctively, Laura leaned away from him, against the back of her seat. She felt powerless and trapped. The man's face was within a few inches from hers.

"Don't be afraid. I want to rescue you."

Rescue her? Rescue her from what?

He's a lunatic. It was the only explanation in her mind. This man was a psycho.

"Please leave," she said in a trembling voice.

"Laura... you have to believe me..."

Laura looked to her left, searching for her agent, but he was far away and watching the scene, a security guard by his side. She caught his eye and gave him an imploring look, and Tougas immediately understood that something was wrong. He touched the guard's shoulder and indicated that he should follow him. Both approached with a quick step.

The man in front of Laura understood that he was going to be taken away and looked at Laura with despair.

"No, no, no, Laura, no. Please listen to me."

The security guard grabbed his right shoulder, but the young man squirmed away from his grip with a quick movement. He was still talking to Laura, but in a louder tone.

"They want to hurt you, Laura. Believe me, you're going to die. Come with me. I'll explain everything to you."

"Sir, come with me. You are blocking everyone," said the security guard in a low voice, holding him firmly by the arm.

The man tried to get out of his grip, but the guard was stronger than him. Tougas attempted to reason with him the best he could, but with limited success. The man was very agitated; he was imploring Laura to listen to him, saying he wanted to clarify something with her. She was terrified but reassured by Tougas' coolness.

Seeing that the man was still fighting back, she got up and walked away so the man could no longer see her. She distinctly heard the crowd shouting insults him. She was sorrier than ever she had not stayed home. The image of the man's soft but tortured eyes haunted her. She was scared, but also felt sorry for him. Some people had serious issues but were not getting the help they needed. She wondered how she could return to her seat after that. She was not comfortable.

It took several minutes for Tougas and Anouk to calm her down and convince her to come back. They put no pressure on her, assuring her that ultimately it was her choice; people would understand. Tougas said that the security guard would remain close to her. Laura hesitated. It seemed unfair for her other fans to be penalized by this incident; finally, she went back to her seat to the sound of cheers from the crowd.

She looked furtively around her and was relieved not to see the man anymore. The security guard was standing at her side now, and he told her that the man had left the scene with the police. She thanked him for his help and smiled at the next person standing in front of her.

4

J immy was distraught. The worst-case scenario had materialized. Not only had he failed to convince Laura to listen to him, but he had frightened her and looked like a maniac. It was over; he wouldn't have a second chance to speak with her. She would never listen to him now that he had scared her. Also, some people had undoubtedly filmed the scene with their cell phones. It will be all over the internet, and he would be a laughingstock. *Look at this asshole freaking out, unable to control himself in front of Laura Labelle.* How was he supposed to cope with that? His only salvation would be through Laura's death, proving to all that he was right. He obviously didn't want her to perish, though; he was doing everything he could to save her life.

He brightened for a moment: since he'd dyed his hair, maybe people wouldn't recognize him once it returned to its natural colour. He just had to wear a cap in the meantime, or shave his head.

The two policewomen had been respectful of him, too, quite a lot more than the security guard. That guy had been on a power trip, and had roughed him up more than necessary. In the end, Jimmy had promised the police that he wouldn't go back to the mall, and that he would no longer harass Laura. He had tried to tell them about the threats against the actress, but the two women didn't believe him either.

No one believed him.

Jimmy had failed again, and once again he felt useless. Him and his grotesque demeanour; him and his dyed hair and his overly loose clothes. Who was he trying to convince? He and Laura were not from the same world and never would be.

As he walked back to his apartment, he stared at the ground. He didn't dare to meet other people's looks. He just wanted to go home and never leave his apartment again. All he had left was the hope that the producers of the show would change their minds and that the plan to kill Laura would fail.

STILL SITTING IN HER SEAT, still signing autographs, Laura kept thinking about what had happened. The man had been warning her of some danger. Was it a threat from him, or had he heard something from someone? She didn't feel good at all, but she did everything in her power to ensure that it didn't show. She had a persistent feeling of nausea that wouldn't leave her.

Fortunately, no one brought the matter up again, and things had returned to normal—or as normal as could be after that kind of shock.

Martine occasionally checked in on her to make sure everything was fine, while her agent watched her with concern, looking at her like a father worried about his daughter. There were only about thirty minutes left before the event was over.

Laura decided she didn't believe the man was out to get her. He'd seemed sincere, although somewhat troubled. She hadn't perceived any malice in his eyes. He had had a strange appearance, but Laura didn't care about how people looked. She had been eccentric herself when she was younger, and if she weren't an actress who needed to have a clean image, she would still have blue hair and darkened eyes.

She thought again about the man's alarmed look when the security guard had subdued him. It was as if he had realized he wouldn't achieve his goals, and that this was somehow dramatic.

Poor guy, she thought. He was probably well-intentioned.

She could hear her mother blaming her for thinking that everyone had a good side, saying that she should be more cautious, that she shouldn't trust people so much. It was true that Laura saw kindness in everyone and that she was too sweet. The decision to hire her former agent was a good illustration of that point. She had believed his bullshit and trusted him fully, thinking that he'd had her best interests at heart. But in the end, he had working for his own wallet and his own fame.

Laura didn't want to admit it, but she was curious to find out what the strange young man wanted to say to her. It was probably a whim, but what if it was true? If she was really in danger?

Suddenly, she felt very vulnerable.

She smiled when she saw that Bruno had arrived and was standing beside Mike Tougas. He waved at her, then turned away and talked to Tougas. After a moment, he turned back to her and gave her a worried look. Apparently, Tougas was referring to what had happened earlier. Bruno talked with Tougas a bit more, then turned and smiled timidly at her and gave her a thumbs up.

After the signing session, she walked over to meet him and kissed him in front of everyone; she didn't care what others thought, or if they thought that Bruno was at the cause of her breakup with François Béliveau. All she cared about was the love she had for him. She took a look at Tougas, who smiled as he looked at them. No judgmental stares. She was reassured.

Tougas walked up to them both. "Look, Laura," he said, "under these circumstances, if you and Bruno would rather postpone tonight's dinner until another day, we'll understand."

Laura had appreciated that Tougas had included Bruno in the discussion. She thought for a moment that she would indeed be more interested in spending the evening alone with her boyfriend, but she had to discuss her future with her agent. She wanted him to understand as soon as possible that her relationship with Bruno was non-negotiable, and she needed the guarantee that not only was it understood, but that he didn't have any concerns with that.

Besides, Bruno seemed willing to eat dinner with them, so she might as well strike while the iron was hot.

"No, it's okay, Mike. I'm a little shaken up, but I want to talk to you about the next steps moving forward. I also want the four of us to get to know each other."

Laura wanted Mike to know that not only should Bruno be included in all the plans he had for her, but that Anouk was also part of the team. Laura enjoyed having Anouk around.

Tougas gave her a radiant smile that made her feel more comfortable. Anouk came up, grabbed her by the shoulders and promised her that they would have a great time. Laura was loosening up already; the hardest part was done. A lovely meal would be welcome.

She didn't know it yet, but the evening wasn't going to be as smooth as she expected.

5

"**W**hat did I tell you, huh? What did I tell you? The gentle approach never works. You should have forced her to follow you, like I told you. But no, you had to do it your way, didn't you?"

Dominic was furious after Jimmy returned and had wasted no time letting him know. He was pacing around the apartment, screaming and gesturing. Dominic already knew that Jimmy had failed before he even told him.

"I knew you were a failure. Now she's going to die. Like Mom. Like Lydia. You're such a loser."

His brother's words tore him apart like a thousand sword strokes in his heart. Jimmy would have appreciated more backing from him.

Dominic left the room, leaving his brother stranded. Jimmy stared at the floor in silence. His head was spinning. The reference to his sister had disturbed him.

Jimmy had somehow become his sister's father figure after their father left the family. It had become more acute when their mother had died a few years later.

Even though they had lived with their aunt, Lydia had idolized her big brother as if he were Jesus Christ. Jimmy had taken care of her, but they had drifted apart when Lydia had become a teenager. Suddenly, she didn't need him anymore. Worse, she didn't want Jimmy to be around her. Lydia would vanish for months without any news, then resurface as if nothing had happened. It pissed Jimmy off, and he had blamed her for not being considerate of those who cared about her.

The two were always arguing, and Lydia would leave, slamming the door behind her. Jimmy was angry with himself each time, but he couldn't tolerate his sister's lack of respect.

Then, finally, after one of these clashes, Lydia had disappeared for good. No more news, no more contact. Jimmy's aunt blamed him for mismanaging the situation, for pushing Lydia away. Who knew if she wasn't under the grip of some pimp, forcing her to prostitute herself, or of other unsavoury people? Without acknowledging it openly, Jimmy also blamed himself. He could have been cleverer at handling the matter. Every time he went outside, he would check around him to see if he might see Lydia. He began strolling through the city's most rotten neighbourhoods, hoping to find her and persuade her to move back with him, into his new apartment.

Nearly three years later, Jimmy was walking alone in town, returning from his job as a journeyman in a factory, when he saw his sister standing on a street corner alongside another girl. Both were apparently prostitutes, harassing bystanders. When Jimmy came closer to her, Lydia froze for a few seconds, then stepped away towards the door of a dingy triplex. Jimmy shouted at his sister to wait for him, he just wanted a word with her, but she fled from him like she was scared to death. Jimmy didn't understand why she was behaving like that. He had never been violent with her. He had always wanted what was best for her. So why would she run away from him like he was a monster?

Her unsteady gait indicated that she was under the influence—drugs or alcohol, or both. He couldn't be sure. The other girl managed to get between him and Lydia, but Jimmy firmly pushed her away and headed into the building after her. He called out to her in a begging voice. An enormous man came down the stairs to meet him, threateningly asking what he wanted.

"She's my sister. Move over," Jimmy said.

The tough guy didn't flinch. "She doesn't want to see you, so get the fuck out."

Jimmy kept climbing up the stairs, but the man stood in the way and tackled him against the wall.

"I'm not going to tell you again, you moron. Get the fuck out of here, or I'll smash your motherfucking head to the ground."

Jimmy tried to push him away, but the man was much stronger than him. He must have been twice his size. Jimmy called out Lydia's name as the man pulled him down the stairs.

Once outside, he kept calling out his sister's name despite the insults of people nearby who were tired of him screaming. Seeing that this was not working, Jimmy left, thinking that he would come back after figuring out a plan to get her to follow him. Lost in his thoughts, he was walking without looking where he was going and heard someone shouting "JIMMY!" He stopped abruptly just before a car rushed past him and headed on its way. Jimmy turned back and saw Lydia standing in a window on the top floor of the three-storey building, looking at him with apprehension.

She had saved his life.

Beckoning to her with his hand, he begged her to come down and talk to him, but the massive man appeared behind her now and grabbed her by the shoulders, and they disappeared. Jimmy stayed there for several minutes, hoping that his sister would come out or come back to the window, but she did neither.

He returned home, glad at least to know where he could find her.

A few weeks later, while on the lookout for her, he saw her enter an apartment building with a man different from the previous one. He ran towards her, but she saw him from the corner of her eye and rushed into the building. He tried to follow her, but the door was locked. He knocked on the door several times but there was no answer.

After about an hour, the man had exited alone, without Lydia. Jimmy asked him where his sister was, and the man told him that Lydia had left several minutes earlier by exiting through the back door. Jimmy had run to find her, but saw no sign of her anywhere. He couldn't figure out why his sister refused to talk to him. He didn't want to judge or denigrate her; he just wanted to do something for her, ask her if she needed anything.

He was all by himself, left to his own devices. He couldn't count on anyone.

A few weeks later, on a cold November evening, his aunt had called him to inform him that the police were trying to reach him. He telephoned the inspector, who asked Jimmy to meet him at the police station right away.

When Jimmy insisted on knowing what it was about, the inspector revealed that Lydia had been found dead. Jimmy's legs buckled. He had cried for several hours before being strong enough to meet with the inspector. He thought he would lose his mind. He thought he'd never make it through, that he was either going to kill himself or go completely insane.

The inspector had asked him to identify the body on the cold metal table in front of him because his aunt didn't have the strength to do it. Jimmy had brought along a plushie that Lydia loved. He didn't know why, but he hoped it would give him some strength.

He had raised his hand to his mouth as the clerk removed

the sheet, revealing the cold, inert face of his little sister. Warm tears had run down his cheeks. She was staring straight ahead, her mouth slightly ajar.

No doubt it was Lydia.

As a formality, he had lifted the sheet to show the corpse's left ankle. Jimmy half-hoped that the little flower tattoo Lydia had gotten for her fifteenth birthday would be missing, but it was there.

Jimmy felt behind him for a chair, as he was about to black out. The officer helped him to sit. Once seated, Jimmy did everything in his power not to lose consciousness. He wept silently, his face buried in Lydia's stuffed toy. The smell of the little teddy bear brought back memories of a happier time with her.

At the front desk, Jimmy collected his sister's personal belongings and threw them in the garbage, except for the three photos inside her wallet. The first picture was of their aunt; there was one of Jimmy when he was about ten years old, and one of Dominic when he was about six.

The forensic examination determined that Lydia had died from a Fentanyl overdose. She had been found the next day, slumped against a waste container in an alleyway, near where Jimmy had last seen her.

With his aunt's assistance, he had arranged Lydia's funeral. He had slipped the teddy bear under her arm just before her coffin was closed.

Her favourite teddy bear was going to accompany her forever.

He had kissed Lydia on the forehead and told her he loved her. He had asked her for forgiveness for failing to figure out a way to save her life. He had escorted the procession to the burial site, supporting his aunt Francine as best as he could.

Francine, who had taken them in after their mother's passing, had never been the same after Lydia's death. She had lapsed into a semi-catatonic state, and Jimmy had reluctantly placed her in a nursing home for the elderly. She was autonomous, but no longer had a passion for anything.

Jimmy took the lead in the discussion when he visited her every week. He made it a point to buy her the latest detective novels by her favourite authors. She loved reading books and watching movies, and spent most days doing only that. Jimmy felt that something had been shattered in their relationship. Although she never overtly criticized him, he knew that his aunt held him responsible for Lydia's death.

Jimmy, for his part, acted as if nothing happened. They had never discussed Lydia's death together after her funeral.

Dominic came back into Jimmy's life shortly after Lydia's death. For Jimmy, it was an overwhelming pleasure to see him again, the man who had been missing from the radar screen for several years. Somehow, Dominic's presence made Lydia's death a little more tolerable. Jimmy had lost a sister but had gotten his brother back. He would rather have had both at the same time, but he would take full advantage of his brother's presence. He wasn't going to make the same mistake he'd made with Lydia.

Dominic had no drug addictions and was not in any dispute with Jimmy; in that sense, they were starting from a blank page. But Dominic wasn't working, saying he was disabled. He had not wanted to elaborate on the reasons for this inability, and Jimmy had agreed to accommodate him at no cost.

Jimmy did everything he could to avoid arguing with his brother. He didn't want him to leave too. Dominic was high maintenance and spent his days looking out the window and voicing his opinion about what Jimmy should or shouldn't do. Sometimes he had good advice; other times not. Jimmy would listen to his brother, but in the end, he did what he wanted.

After Jimmy got home from the fiasco at the mall, he picked up the phone.

"What are you doing?" Dominic said as he approached him.

"I'm telling Mathieu I'm not going to meet him at the restaurant tonight."

"And let him laugh at you because you failed to get with Laura? No. You're going to go and tell him that, unfortunately, Laura couldn't make it tonight but that you're going to get it together. You need to look confident."

"I'm really not in the mood for this, Dom."

Dominic burst out, "I don't give a shit what you want or not. You're going to man up and get to the restaurant, handle the situation."

He looked strange; his face had dark spots on it, and his eyes were bulging.

"Calm down," Jimmy told him. "The neighbours will hear us. I'm going to go, all right. But be quiet."

Dominic calmed down. "Finally, some sense. Jimmy is growing a pair."

"Come with me," Jimmy said.

"No."

Jimmy gritted his teeth. He was irritated by his brother's reclusive life, but Dominic would get angry when he brought it up. He said that he lived his life as he saw fit and that if he wanted to spend his days indoors without seeing anyone, he would. Dominic had no friends; he had been gone for too long and had no desire to rebuild a new social life—especially since he saw how people treated Jimmy, how they marginalized him. These people didn't deserve his friendship.

"Okay, fine," Jimmy said. "I get it. Just stay here. I don't give a shit."

Dominic left the room in a fury. He grabbed his coat, saying he needed to get some fresh air.

Jimmy placed his phone on the living room table and sighed as he dropped onto the couch. He really didn't want to go out tonight. The dust would settle, and Dominic would let it go. Jimmy picked up his phone again and texted, "I won't be here tonight. Sorry."

Mathieu would understand. Never mind if he was laughing at him about Laura. He didn't care. Nothing mattered now that he had failed.

~

LAURA WAS PLEASED with the vibe that prevailed in the taxi carrying the two couples to the restaurant. The discussion flowed smoothly. Bruno got along fine with Mike Tougas, which was the harbinger of a promising business relationship between the agent and his star.

With all this, Laura had almost forgotten the unfortunate events that had taken place at the beginning of the evening. Or rather, she did everything she could to not think about it. It just freaked her out and made her feel uncomfortable. It was over now, though, she told herself. Let's move on.

They were greeted by the hostess and were given a place near a window. Tougas had asked for a table that was a little further away so that they could talk. Nevertheless, Laura expected they would be disrupted by fans a few times during the meal. It was during these moments that Laura missed the time when she had not been well known and could go anywhere she wanted without being stopped by her admirers. In fact, she hated just about everything that came with her acting job except the acting itself. She would have been fine without the rest.

Her relationship with François Béliveau had convinced her to stop disclosing too much about her personal life in the media. She didn't want to be one of those hypocrites who appeared on magazine covers to celebrate their love, but when they broke up, asked people to leave them alone to deal with their pain.

Tougas had no problem with Laura's demands. Bruno agreed. He didn't want to be recognized either. All that mattered was the love they had for each other.

The waiter suggested drinks before the meal. Tougas asked for the wine list. Although Laura was not a wine enthusiast, she didn't mind her agent's offer to order a bottle of red wine. Bruno was fond of wine and recommended some bottles for consideration. The waiter gave them a few minutes to decide and headed back to the kitchen. Given that the waiter hadn't made any reference to her presence, Laura figured that either he didn't know her or he didn't care about her presence. Regardless, Laura appreciated the restraint because it was not always the case.

"A bottle of pinot noir, then?" Tougas asked Bruno.

"Yes, I'm okay with that. Laura?"

She shrugged; she didn't know the difference between a pinot noir and a chardonnay.

Tougas ordered the bottle. Laura took the floor.

"I'm glad we are all together right now," she said. "The reason I dumped my other agent was that he wanted to control my relationships and tell me how to live my life."

"He's the one behind your relationship with Béliveau, isn't he?" said Tougas with a smile.

Laura was surprised that it was so obvious. She wavered for a few seconds before answering positively, lowering her eyes. Tougas grabbed her hand.

"He does that with everyone, Laura. You don't have to be embarrassed by that. Suffice it to say, it's not my style." He let go of her hand and straightened up like a salesman starting his sales pitch. "With us, the client dictates the direction she wants her career to go, not the other way around. I have clients who know very well where they are going and what they want to accomplish; others ask us to take charge of their destiny and guide them to the best of our ability. In both cases, we do our best, but in the end, the artist's choice prevails."

Laura was happy to hear this, but wondered if what he was saying was true. Maybe it was just a strategy to gain her confidence and then, quietly, get control.

She noticed that Bruno seemed content with what he was hearing. She was willing to give Tougas a chance.

The agent noticed that Laura was doubtful. "Do you know Isabelle Masson?"

"Of course. She is my favourite singer," Laura said.

"Do you believe she's married?"

Laura didn't know.

"Who is her spouse? How many children does she have?"

After reflection, Laura admitted that she had no idea.

"No wonder you don't know," Tougas said, "because she doesn't want anyone to know. She wants to be known only for her songs. She is married to an accountant working for a music label and has two children, eight and six years old.

"She's my client. I never pushed her to disclose more than she wanted. I never tried to change her mind. I respected her wishes. You never see her in gossip magazines. You only rarely see her in talk shows, and when she appears on those, she speaks exclusively about her new album. I make it clear right away with the show hosts that she won't talk about her private life, and they respect that."

Laura was reassured and smiled. Obviously, she had made the right choice. She settled into her chair and finally relaxed for the first time in several weeks. Bruno put his hand gently on her thigh and smiled at her. Everything was fine.

"Now," Mike Tougas said after finishing his glass of wine. "What do you want to do? Where do you see yourself in five or ten years?"

6

Jimmy was sitting silently. The television was turned off; there was no sound in the apartment except for noises coming from the street. Dominic hadn't returned from his walk. Jimmy had observed other shadows moving quickly around him but didn't care anymore because it was happening so frequently now. Probably something wrong with his eyes. Wasn't seeing shadows a symptom of cataracts? He had never had any before, but he thought it was something like that.

He noticed that his cell phone was vibrating. He looked at the display. The call was coming from the Deux Cigognes restaurant. It was obviously Mathieu, wanting to talk to him, but Jimmy didn't have the energy to do so and didn't feel like hearing Mathieu pulling his chains about Laura. The phone finally stopped buzzing, but after a few minutes of silence, Jimmy noticed there was no envelope icon in the upper left corner of the screen. Mathieu had not left a message. It probably wasn't important. Jimmy knew that, one day, he would have to face Mathieu's comments about Laura, but not now. He was not in the right state of mind.

"What did he want?"

Jimmy jumped when he heard Dominic's voice behind him.

"Jesus Christ, Dominic, you scared the shit out of me. I didn't hear you coming back."

"What did he want?"

Jimmy stared at his brother: the black spots on his face were spreading like gangrene. "Dominic, we have to do something, man. You have black spots all over your face."

Dominic laughed. "You're still a hypochondriac, brother?"

Jimmy was puzzled. Why wasn't he worried about this? He was surprised to see a shadow quickly passing behind his brother. Shit, he was truly hallucinating.

"I'm going crazy, Dom."

"It's that bitch, Laura."

Jimmy stood up. How dare he? "Shut the fuck up, Dominic. She had nothing to do with it. I'm the idiot who didn't know how to get my message across. How would you have reacted in her position if you had seen me show up in front of you, without warning, telling you to follow me? Look at me, for heaven's sake, with my hair dyed like a loser. I had no credibility."

Dominic glared at him. Jimmy knew what he was thinking. Dominic had already told him he was weak, too kind.

Jimmy sat down on the couch again, turning his back to him. Dominic didn't know Laura as well as he did. She was innocent and pure. She wasn't a bad person. Dominic couldn't understand.

Jimmy's phone vibrated again. He sighed and looked at the notification on his screensaver. It was a text message from Mathieu. "Call me ASAP. You'll never believe who's here."

Jimmy's mind raced as he dialled his friend's phone number.

What if it was Laura?

JIMMY STOOD outside the front door of the restaurant, hesitant to enter. He was as anxious as he had been earlier in the day, just before talking to Laura. He had put a cap on his head and changed his clothes.

Mathieu had told him that Laura was with three other people he didn't know. When Jimmy told him he was coming, Mathieu made him promise not to do anything to embarrass him. Jimmy assured him that he only wanted to check that everything was fine.

At Dominic's insistence, Jimmy had slipped his Glock between his lower back and his belt. It was for his protection, he told himself, but he didn't intend to use it. He had acquired this gun after Lydia's death because he feared for his safety. Word on the street was that some men from a gang were looking for him.

Ultimately, he had never had any problems with anyone from organized crime, and he had gradually stopped dragging his gun everywhere with him. Nevertheless, he'd kept it, in case he needed it one day.

Mathieu had told Jimmy that Laura was with an older couple and a young man in his early thirties. This man looked like her new boyfriend, Mathieu said.

Impossible, Jimmy thought. She had just broken up with François Béliveau. She wasn't going to throw herself on the first person to come along. It wasn't her style.

As Jimmy walked through the door, he scanned the place and spotted Laura with the trio on his right, sitting at a table away from him. He didn't notice Mathieu right away. He must have been in the kitchen. The hostess approached him.

"Hi, Jimmy. Are you all right?"

Jimmy smiled shyly at her. There were not many customers in the restaurant tonight; he would have preferred to blend in more easily with the crowd. But that was to be expected. The restaurant was not very busy on Wednesday nights. That's why Jimmy had picked this day to come and see his friend, figuring he'd have more time to talk to him.

He sat down at the table designated by the hostess. At first, she wanted him to sit more to the right side of the dining room, but it was too close to Laura for his liking, so he moved to a secluded table near the bar. Mathieu greeted him a few minutes later, smiling, and made a derogatory remark about how right he was. Laura Labelle was indeed in the restaurant, as he had promised.

"Just not with you," he said, laughing.

Jimmy's face flushed with a mixture of rage and shame. "Do you think that's funny, Mathieu?"

Mathieu stopped giggling when he saw how angry Jimmy was. "Come on, I'm just teasing you. Calm down."

"I'm not in the mood for that kind of bullshit tonight," said Jimmy.

Without a word, Mathieu headed back to the kitchen, wishing he hadn't called Jimmy. He didn't seem to be in his right mind about her. Mathieu had a bad feeling about this. Why was Jimmy here, in this state of mind? He decided he would allow him to chill for a few minutes; he'd go and sit with him to make sure he didn't have any harmful intentions.

Jimmy looked at Laura with a keen eye, trying to hide his face under his cap the best he could. She hadn't seen him. Or if she had seen him, she didn't recognize him. It was perfect. He wanted to find out who the other three people were.

He recognized the older man sitting across from her; it was the guy who had tried to reason with him when that fucking security guard had grabbed him so cavalierly earlier in the day. He was confident that it was Laura's new agent. On the other hand, the elegant woman next to him didn't ring a bell; she was most likely his wife or a colleague. Anyway, Jimmy was more concerned by the young man to Laura's right. He worried that Mathieu was right, given their complicit smiles and the way they kept running their hands over each other. Maybe it was Laura's new boyfriend, maybe her rebound. In both cases, Jimmy felt an intense burn of envy filling his chest.

He was also disappointed by Laura. Perhaps she was the kind of person to move from one man to another after all.

Immediately to his right, a shadow quickly passed by, and Jimmy turned his head away. He was increasingly irritated by what he now considered to be hallucinations. As soon as Laura was involved, the shadows would emerge.

Jimmy didn't have time to expand on the subject; he was dumbfounded to see his brother Dominic sitting at a table at the back of the restaurant. He gestured to ask him what he was doing there, but Dominic ignored him, staring at Laura's party without shame. He will screw it up, Jimmy thought while getting up to approach him.

"What the hell are you doing here?" Jimmy said.

Dominic had a mean grin. "I'm going to make sure you do what you have to do."

His face was completely black now, like he had just come out of a coal mine.

"You're all dirty. Go home. You'll draw attention."

Dominic looked into his brother's eyes, and his expression felt like a massive blow to Jimmy's chest. He turned his attention to Laura's table. "Do you have any bullets in your gun?"

Jimmy couldn't figure out why his brother was so agitated. What was going on with him? What was he going to do, for heaven's sake?

Jimmy asked him to be quiet, and went back to his seat.

Mathieu came to join him. "What's going on, Jimmy? You seem upset."

"It's all right. It's my brother again."

Mathieu sighed. "What has he done now?"

Jimmy waved at him to drop it and turned to look at Laura. The four were eating now, laughing and joking. Clearly, they hadn't noticed Dominic watching them. He had at least had the decency to sit in a less well-lit corner of the restaurant.

"Jimmy, I'm sorry about earlier," Mathieu said. "I didn't mean to offend you. I didn't know it was such a sensitive subject for you."

He didn't know? How could he not have seen Jimmy's love for Laura, his devotion to her? Jimmy had mentioned to him several times that she was the woman of his dreams, the perfect one.

But right now, Jimmy didn't want to be noticed, so he told Mathieu that everything was fine. He also apologized for his outburst.

After a few minutes of silence, Mathieu asked him the question that had been bothering him since their dispute. "You won't do anything inappropriate, will you, Jimmy?" He immediately regretted the words he had chosen. It had come out wrong. He didn't mean that Jimmy was out of place; he just wanted to make sure he wasn't going to do anything unexpected.

Although Jimmy stiffened up before answering the question, he reassured his friend that he was only there to see what was going to happen. He refrained from sharing his concerns about Dominic. Jimmy was on the alert; if Dominic tried anything stupid, he'd intervene. Otherwise, he would sit there until the group left. Laura was clearly having fun. She wasn't in any imminent danger. Jimmy relaxed a little and ordered a beer.

~

THE EVENING HAD BEEN GOING WELL, and Laura was thrilled. The four of them were clicking very well, and she was happy she had decided to come to the restaurant and discuss things forthrightly with her agent. Things were clear now. Everyone knew where they stood. She had explained how she had trouble with public appearances, such as signing sessions, and that she wanted to limit them as much as possible. She knew she could never convince the producers of the show not to make her take part in them again, and she didn't want to put her agent in a difficult spot. Laura had also mentioned that she would like to play a role at the other end of the spectrum from the one she played in the show. She would like to play a villain, a criminal, something that would take her out of her comfort zone and show another side of her to the public.

Mike Tougas had smiled and said that he might have something in mind. He had heard about an upcoming role of a female prisoner in a television series featuring an actress that the public adored. Laura was excited about this prospect. Tougas was the opposite of her other agent. He always had the perfect answers to her questions.

The restaurant was tranquil tonight. There were few people, and there was jazz music playing brightly in the background. As she watched the small number of customers at the restaurant, she saw their waiter in a discussion with a lonely man wearing a cap. The waiter had glanced at them a few times and then turned his attention away. Obviously, the two of them knew each other, and the waiter knew who Laura was. The client wearing the cap looked at her a few times as well, but that was normal for Laura. People recognized her and glanced at her from time to time.

She appreciated when people respected her privacy by allowing her to enjoy her meal without talking to her.

"Can I get you a coffee or dessert?" the waiter asked when he returned to their table.

Anouk and Laura looked at each other for a moment with a smile, each waiting for the other to speak first. Eventually,

Anouk requested the dessert menu and a cappuccino. Everyone had a coffee except Bruno, who asked for another Perrier. He was concerned, although he did everything in his power to be part of the discussions. What Tougas had told him earlier in the day about the lunatic and Laura had been worrying him ever since. She told him several times that there was nothing to worry about. Yes, she had been rather alarmed, but she had not felt threatened physically; it was more the man's behaviour that had shaken her. Bruno understood that as a celebrity, Laura was a prime target for those crazy people who might mistake their desires for reality. How many stories had there been of madmen who had successfully entered American celebrities' homes? Laura was not immune to all this.

"People make up all kinds of things to be interesting," Bruno had told her, to comfort her.

"I know."

But right now, the man in the cap made Bruno uncomfortable. He kept looking in their direction, even if he was trying to be subtle. The server seemed to know the man, as he talked to him more often than wait staff would typically do with a regular customer.

"Excuse me," Bruno said to the waiter, who had returned with the beverages. "Do you know that guy? The one with the cap on?"

Mathieu turned for a moment and looked at Jimmy. "Yes, he's a regular customer. Why?"

"No reason."

Tougas was caught off guard by Bruno's question, and by his suspicious look. Bruno told him he was fine, that he was just on his guard, given today's events. Laura appreciated that her boyfriend was worried about her, but she decided to change the topic by asking Tougas and Anouk how they'd met.

Tougas allowed Anouk to tell the story and excused himself to go to the bathroom. He walked by the gentleman in the cap, who was facing away from him. Tougas greeted a patron he knew on his way and opened the bathroom door.

Upon his return, Tougas smiled at the bartender, and said, "Quiet evening, huh?" She nodded. It was indeed quiet, even for a Wednesday evening.

Tougas slowly passed by the man sitting by himself once again, and this time, the man looked up at him before promptly dropping his head once more.

Tougas felt dizzy as he recognized him. He wandered back to his table, wondering what to do.

"Are you all right?" Laura asked.

Tougas hesitated for a few seconds. He mustn't cause Laura to panic. Everyone was looking at him, concerned. Anouk asked him what was wrong with him.

He opted to be transparent. "I don't want you guys to freak out, but we may have a situation."

Laura stiffened in her chair. She didn't know Mike Tougas well, but his anxious expression made her very nervous.

Tougas was searching for the right words. "The man from this afternoon, the one we had to drag out from the mall—"

Laura didn't need to hear anything more; she understood right away. She looked at the man, who was looking at her. Immediately, he turned his eyes away like a child caught misbehaving.

"Let's go," she said, and got to her feet. Tougas agreed. He and Bruno and Anouk rose, as Tougas was taking care of the bill.

Laura set off towards the door, then turned to see Bruno moving decisively towards the man.

"Bruno," Laura hissed.

"What the hell is he doing?" Tougas asked.

She hoped he wouldn't attempt to be a hero.

Bruno stood in front of the man, who ignored him, still staring at his plate.

7

Jimmy was mad at himself.

His gaze was drawn to someone passing by his table, and as he looked up out of reflex, he found himself staring at Laura Labelle's agent. Within seconds, the agent had lost his smile, and his pupils had dilated. Jimmy knew he'd recognized him, and that it was time for him to leave. He glanced at Laura, who looked back at him with fear. He waved at Mathieu to bring him the bill.

Jimmy looked towards Dominic, who shook his head to show his displeasure. He was looking at him as if he was the dumbest of cretins. Jimmy ignored him. Perhaps he was mistaken; perhaps Tougas had only been frightened by his looks. Maybe he had only imagined the fear in the agent's eyes, just as he imagined the shadows spinning around him all the time now.

The density of the shadows intensified every second, so much so that Jimmy had trouble spotting his brother. He was still there, but now he was nothing more than a black shade. The only things that stood out on Dominic's face were his eyes, like protruding white balls. Jimmy rubbed his own eyes a little;

there was something wrong with them. Maybe he was going blind. How could it be that his vision was deteriorating so rapidly? The shadows danced around him in a grotesque choreographed pattern.

Jimmy sensed someone standing next to him. Moments ago, he had heard a panicked voice in the distance but hadn't heard what it said. From the corner of his eye, Jimmy now recognized that the man beside him had been the one sitting next to Laura at her table.

Jimmy ignored him, even though the man spoke to him in an angry tone. Mathieu showed up now, frightened, and begged the man not to bother the guests. As Bruno instructed Mathieu to keep his mouth shut, Jimmy heard Dominic bossing him to do something.

"Are you going to let a complete nobody insult the only friend you have in life? Get up, you coward."

Jimmy felt rage building up in him, a rage like he had never experienced before. He looked at Mathieu, who was still struggling to convince the other man to leave him alone. Some of the customers had grabbed their coats and rushed out of the restaurant, sensing that something was going to go wrong. Bruno moved closer to Mathieu as if he intended to harm him.

"Call the police," Mathieu told the bartender.

Tougas hurried up to Bruno now, urging him to cool down and let it go.

Then Jimmy heard Bruno insult him, calling him an asshole who was only good at threatening women.

"Get up, Jimmy, for heaven's sake!" Dominic shouted. "Will you shut him up, or do I have to step in?"

As if an outside force was lifting him, Jimmy got up and pulled his Glock out from behind his back.

"No, Jimmy!" shouted Mathieu.

But Jimmy was already pointing the barrel of the gun towards Bruno's face.

"So, what are you going to do now?" Jimmy sneered. "What are you going to do now, you asshole?"

Bruno took a few steps backward, raising his hands slightly. He looked at Jimmy with a mixture of fear and hate.

"Jimmy, what the hell are you doing?" Mathieu cried. "The police are on their way. You don't have to do this."

"Are you all right, Matt?" Jimmy asked, keeping Bruno in check.

"Yes, I'm fine, but please drop the gun."

Jimmy heard his brother's voice behind him; he was still sitting at his table. "This is your moment, Jimmy. What you couldn't do when you had your first chance, you can do now. You can talk to Laura. You can help her understand what's coming for her. This is your moment. Grab it."

"Everyone out, except for Laura," Jimmy ordered. "Mathieu, make sure you get the clients and the staff out. Everyone but Laura."

"Don't do anything stupid, Jimmy," Mathieu said. "Please send everyone out."

"I said everyone but Laura," Jimmy shouted, diverting his attention from Bruno for a few seconds.

Bruno seized his opportunity and jumped on him in an attempt to disarm him. But he had tackled him improperly, like a football player, by wrapping his arms around Jimmy's torso. Jimmy tumbled backwards and temporarily lost control of his gun. The two men crashed onto Jimmy's table, knocking the half-full beer bottle and the empty plates off it.

Bruno somehow managed to climb over Jimmy by pushing him down with his hands on his shoulders, but with a sharp motion, Jimmy turned to his left and pushed Bruno back enough to free his right arm.

Jimmy saw that Tougas was scrambling for the gun. With a superhuman effort, he pushed his assailant away with a knee blow to the sides that made Bruno bend in half. Then Jimmy hurled himself to his right, rolled twice and grabbed his gun. Tougas braked sharply and stepped back and raised his hands as he saw Jimmy holding him at gunpoint.

"Well done, Jimmy. I'm proud of you. Well done!" Dominic shouted, jumping up and down as if Jimmy had just won an Olympic gold medal.

Jimmy turned to Bruno. "You won't get another chance to jump me, you stupid bastard." He pointed the gun at Bruno's chest, but at the last moment, he diverted the muzzle to the floor and pulled the trigger.

The gunshot shattered Bruno's foot and he collapsed to the ground, screaming.

Laura rushed over and threw herself on her boyfriend. "Bruno! Are you all right, Bruno?" She gave Jimmy a hateful glare. "You fucking lunatic, what do you want from me? What the hell do you want from me, for God's sake?"

Jimmy felt his heart disintegrating into a thousand pieces. Rarely had words hurt him so much. Laura's tone had devastated him. She despised him deeply. Jimmy had never thought anyone would look at him with such disdain.

"Kill her," Dominic said.

Jimmy quietly watched Bruno writhing in pain and Laura crying.

"This is my fight, Dominic. Not yours."

"I just want to help you, but okay. Do as you wish. After all, that has been so successful for you so far," Dominic mocked back.

Jimmy asked Mathieu to assist in taking Bruno out and repeated that everyone should leave except Laura.

"I won't go out without her," said Tougas.

Jimmy pointed his gun towards the man's chest.

"You're crazy," Mike Tougas said.

Jimmy shook his head. "I'm not crazy. I only need to talk to

Laura, that's all. If you'd let me talk to her earlier, all this wouldn't be happening. Now get the fuck out."

"I'm not leaving without her."

Jimmy laughed. "It's not your decision, pal. You either leave on your own, or on a stretcher—your call. I don't care. I have nothing to lose."

Jimmy heard Dominic whistling in admiration behind him.

"Mike, please go," Laura begged him. "He's already shot Bruno, so obviously he can do the same to all of us. Please, get out."

Tougas attempted to reason with his client, but Laura repeated to him that he had to leave. Like everyone else.

"Don't hurt her, you motherfucker," Tougas said to Jimmy as he walked away. "I swear to God, if you do anything to her, I'm going to chase you for the rest of my life until I kill you."

"We have a fucking superhero here," laughed Dominic.

Jimmy smiled and waved at the agent to leave.

"You'll see if I'm a superhero," Tougas muttered as he left with his wife.

Jimmy turned to Mathieu. "Has everyone gone out?"

"Yes," said the waiter, who was weeping. "except for these two and us."

"Perfect," said Jimmy. "Close all the blinds. Lock all the doors except the main entrance and give me the keys."

Mathieu did so, while Jimmy continued to hold Laura and Bruno at gunpoint.

The shadows danced around Jimmy faster than ever, but strangely enough, he could now see clearly through them.

Mathieu returned and handed him two silver keys. "It's done," he said.

"Thank you. I'm sorry, Mathieu. I didn't come here to cause any trouble. I wouldn't have done anything if that idiot hadn't picked on me. You must believe me."

Laura looked at Bruno, who closed his eyes. He had screwed

up. He knew it. But when he opened his eyes, he saw not reproaches in his girlfriend's eyes but rather disappointment mixed with gratitude. She was so composed.

"Help this asshole out," Jimmy told Mathieu, indicating Bruno, "and don't come back."

Mathieu was torn apart, overwhelmed. This sort of thing never ended well, he knew. Jimmy had crossed a line and couldn't go back.

Mathieu leaned down to help Bruno stand up. He passed the young man's arm behind his neck and lifted him so that he could move forward, jumping on one leg. Blood droplets followed them to the door.

"Stay there," Jimmy ordered Laura, and followed the two.

Mathieu handed Bruno to Tougas, who was waiting outside, and turned to Jimmy. "You're a good guy, Jimmy. Don't ever forget that."

Jimmy smiled at him, then shut the door and locked it.

Laura had sat on a chair and was looking at the floor. Jimmy approached her quietly and pulled up a chair to face her.

"I don't want to hurt you," Jimmy told her.

"Too late," Laura replied in an angry tone.

Jimmy took the hit. "The police will be here any minute. They'll take care of your friend."

She laughed, but didn't reply.

Dominic got up and approached his brother.

"We're wasting our time. She doesn't want to understand. Kill that slut and let's move on."

Jimmy looked at his brother in astonishment. "What are you talking about? I'm doing this so that she doesn't die. I'm not going to kill her. You don't make any sense, Dom."

Laura stared at Jimmy with a squeamish look on her face.

He reassured her. "I told you I didn't want to hurt you. I just want to talk to you."

Laura looked at him for a moment, resigned. "I don't really have a choice, do I? So talk."

Jimmy sighed deeply. Everything had not gone as he wanted, but she was there, and he was finally going to tell her what he knew. He took his cap off his head and placed it on the table to his right. He ruffled his bleached blond hair and began his speech, which he had rehearsed at least a hundred times, alone, in front of his mirror.

8

Mike Tougas was pacing, while Bruno complained about the pain in his foot.

"What are the cops doing, for God's sake?" Anouk asked.

"I don't know. What did you tell them when you called?" Mike asked Mathieu.

Mathieu said that a colleague had called 911, not him. She was gone, as were the clients. Only he, Tougas, Anouk and Bruno stood outside now. Tougas was trying to see what was going on inside, but since all the curtains were drawn, he couldn't see a thing.

"Shit, I'll call them back," Tougas said, grabbing his phone. "Yes, hello? Someone called you several minutes ago about a fight at the restaurant Aux Deux Cigognes, and there is still no one here. What are you doing? There's a fucking hostage incident happening right now. Are you going to send someone over? I'm calm, ma'am, but my client is inside with a raging maniac who has a gun. No, I'm not staying on the line. Send someone, and send an ambulance. There's a wounded man here. The psycho shot him in the foot. Hurry the hell up before it's too late."

Tougas hung up the phone. He planned to call back every five minutes if necessary. He and turned to Bruno. "How are you holding up?"

Bruno shook his head and winced. Mathieu had put a tourniquet around his foot, made from a piece of his apron. Bruno kept pressure on the wound, but it hurt him terribly. Mathieu was a little worried about the young man's general appearance; his pale complexion didn't look right.

A few minutes later, three police cars roared in. One car skidded to a halt and stopped sideways on the road. Another passed the group to do the same thing at the other intersection, and then a third car stopped in front of them. Two policemen jumped out with weapons in their hands. Tougas went towards them.

"Good evening, gentlemen. There's an armed man inside, holding actress Laura Labelle hostage. He asked everyone to leave and stayed inside with her."

Hearing moans behind him, one of the police officers signalled his colleague to go and inquire about the man sitting further away.

"What does he want with her?" the first policeman asked.

"I don't know," Tougas replied.

"To talk to her," Mathieu said.

The officer turned to him. "Talk to her?"

"Yes. Just to talk to her."

The cop looked at him for a few seconds. "Couldn't he call her?"

Mathieu shrugged. "If it were that simple. Something happened earlier. This gentleman can probably tell you more," Mathieu said, pointing at Mike Tougas with his chin.

After the officer reported the situation to the dispatcher and asked for a mediator to handle the hostage-taking, he noted Mike Tougas' account of the events earlier in the afternoon.

Bruno refused to leave with the paramedics, but Tougas told him he needed to go to the hospital to take care of his foot. He didn't seem to be doing very well. Tougas promised to keep him informed by text message and after a moment, Bruno agreed to leave with the paramedics.

LAURA HAD LISTENED to Jimmy's nonsensical story and stared at him without a word. The producers wanted her dead? What a load of crap.

"Is that why you're doing all this? On a hunch about a supposed plot to kill me? Where do you think we are? In Russia? It doesn't make any sense."

Jimmy was disappointed that he couldn't find the right words to persuade her.

Laura wondered how she could get out of this mess. Should she pretend to trust him? Or maybe try to reason with him? She had great difficulty decoding this man. She felt that he was looking out for her, but at times, he would become belligerent —breathing hard, tightening his jaw, his eyes filling with fury. Her goal was to keep him as calm as possible, not to upset him.

"Look, I don't know who told you that, but I swear I'm not in any danger."

Jimmy smiled, but he knew she was wrong. "Laura, I'm sorry I can't find the right words to make you understand, but yes, you are in danger. I can't tell you how I know that. But I know that." He knew he couldn't simply tell her that he'd discovered the plot to kill her through his dreams and through clues gathered here and there in the TV show.

The longer he looked at her, the more gorgeous he thought she was. Laura was more beautiful in person than on television.

However, he found he wasn't as intimidated by her as he had been when looking at her pictures. She exuded a heartwarming kindness.

"Get a room, for heaven's sake," Dominic said as he got up. "What are we doing here, Jimmy? You're smitten by her, while —newsflash!—the police are out there, probably with snipers ready to smash your skull to pieces as soon as they have the chance. What do you think's gonna happen—you guys are gonna walk out of here hand in hand? Live happily ever after and have many children? Wake up, you moron."

Jimmy's phone rang. It was an unknown number.

"Well, there you go," Dominic said. "The police. Congratulations!" He ripped the phone out of Jimmy's hands. "I'll take care of public relations. Anyway, you'd stutter like an asshole and get shortchanged by them." He turned to Laura. "And you keep your big mouth shut."

Dominic took the call. "Yes."

"Hi, is this Jimmy?"

"No, it's Dominic."

"Dominic?"

Mathieu looked at the officer.

Fuck.

The moderator raised one arm as he looked towards Mathieu, meaning "What's going on?" He would have to roll with the punches.

"Hello, Dominic. I'm Paul Ménard, sergeant with the Montréal Police Department. Can you put Jimmy on the phone for me?"

"No, Jimmy's busy right now. I'm in charge here."

"All right, Dominic. I want to confirm some information with you." Paul Ménard wrote something in his notebook, snatched it and held it out to Mathieu. "Who's in there besides the two of you?"

"Laura Labelle."

"The actress?"

"Exactly."

Mathieu read Ménard's message; he had written, "family??"

"And what is your relation to them?"

"I'm Jimmy's brother."

"I see. Who shot Bruno Lamarre?"

"The asshole who got a bullet in his foot? That was Jimmy. Although, if it had been me, he wouldn't have been shot in the foot. That jackass. He would be dead by now."

"What's Jimmy doing right now?"

"Enough talk now. We have other things to worry about."

"One last question for now. What do you want with Laura Labelle?"

"To talk to her."

"That's all?"

"Yes."

"Why didn't you call her?"

Dominic hung up.

Mike Tougas approached Paul Ménard. "So?"

"There's another person inside with them."

"Who?"

"Jimmy's brother."

"That means he was hiding somewhere. They had planned this."

Tougas became even more worried. He thought that Jimmy had reacted badly because of Bruno. But if his brother was his accomplice, then this whole thing had been premeditated. This was much more problematic.

Ménard went over to Mathieu. "So?"

"I know he has a brother who has a terrible influence on him, case in point again today. And he has an aunt."

"Do you have her contact information?"

"No."

"Do you know her name?"

"Francine Dion, I think."

"Do you know for sure?"

"I'm pretty sure her name is Francine Dion because I asked him jokingly if she was related to Celine."

Ménard snapped his fingers at one of his colleagues and asked him to contact all the Francine Dions he could find. "Did his brother enter the restaurant with Jimmy?" he said, turning back to Mathieu.

"No," said Mathieu. "Jimmy was alone at his table."

Ménard looked at Mathieu suspiciously.

"What do you mean he was alone? Where was Dominic?"

"I don't know. Maybe he was sitting alone somewhere else. I haven't seen him. Actually, Jimmy has never introduced me to him. He used to talk to me about him a lot, but said he was a homebody."

"Were you alone on duty tonight?"

"No. Another waitress was working on a different section."

"Okay, I want to talk to her."

"She's not here. She left with the others."

"Call her."

"Her contact information is in the restaurant. I'm not the manager. We have a phone list inside."

Ménard sighed. He redialled Jimmy's phone number, but no one answered. The call went straight to voicemail. He tried another time, and this time a male voice answered.

"We'll call you when there's something to tell you."

"I want to talk to Laura, check on her. Make sure she's okay."

The call was cut off.

~

LAURA LOOKED for a way to soften Jimmy up. She didn't believe the murder plot shenanigan about her, but if Jimmy did, maybe she should pretend to go along with it.

She had been through an entire range of emotions in the last half-hour. One moment she thought he would release her; the next moment, she thought she was going to die. It was difficult for her to understand how to deal with this psychopath. Moreover, she was worried sick about Bruno. Had he received the necessary care? Keeping calm took all her energy.

"Your name is Jimmy, right?" she called to him.

It was the first time Laura had mentioned his name. It was like music to his ears. "Yes. And this is Dominic."

Laura abstained from reacting. "I'm worried about my friend, the one who was hurt. When you speak to the police again, can you ask them if he's all right?"

"Dumb bitch," Dominic said. "If I had fired the shot, your son-of-a-bitch boyfriend would have died. I hope he's bleeding to death."

"Careful, Dom," Jimmy shouted as he got up from his chair. "That is not necessary. Just ask them if he's okay, that's all."

Dominic looked at his brother with such contempt that Jimmy looked down.

"You're so helpless. Will I have to kill that bitch? Is that it? You won't do it?"

Laura panicked for a few seconds, but she kept her composure. She had to find a way to bring down the pressure. She didn't want Jimmy to be confused; she had to ensure that he stood up against this Dominic, whoever he was. She couldn't just ignore him.

Clearly, Jimmy liked her and didn't wish her any harm. However, the other guy had the power to seize control and kill her.

"I apologize, Jimmy."

He sat down again. "Excuse me?"

"I'm sorry. I reacted badly to what you told me. It's just. . . it was a surprise, you know? It is tough to accept that those producers would want me dead. I worked every day with these people, but maybe you're right. You want to protect me, and I appreciate that."

Laura waited for Jimmy's reaction, and his face softened reassuringly. She was on to something. She had to carry on in that direction—not contradicting him, acknowledging that his dedication touched her. Make him look like a hero and show appreciation for his willingness to protect her. It was crucial to ensure that the situation would not escalate. She needed to buy more time. As time passed, she figured her chances of getting out of it were better. If she could talk to him and restrict Dominic's outbursts, she might convince him to let her go.

She jolted when the phone rang again. Jimmy looked at the number. It was his aunt. He picked up the phone this time.

"Yes?"

"Jimmy? What the hell are you doing?"

"Excuse me?"

"The police just called me and told me you took somebody hostage. Tell me that's not true?"

He did not answer.

"Jimmy, listen to me. Please, release your hostage. I'll help you. We'll find you some care. It's not too late. You haven't done anything serious yet. Let her go."

"Hang up," Dominic said.

Jimmy looked at his brother speechlessly.

"Hang up the phone!"

"I'm sorry, Auntie, but I can't. I have to protect Laura, but I don't know how yet."

Jimmy heard his aunt sniffing like she was crying. It broke his heart.

"At least allow the police to talk to Laura. Collaborate with them."

"Dominic is talking to them. I'll tell him."

"Dominic? But Jimmy..."

"I have to hang up now. I'm sorry I've hurt your feelings."

Jimmy hung up and put the phone next to him. He noticed that Laura was also crying. He was hurting the women he loved. Dominic was right; he was soft.

Like a good actress, Laura could cry on command. When she noticed that Jimmy felt guilty about his aunt crying, she started to cry herself. If she had to use her acting skills to get out of this mess, she would.

She was playing the most significant role of her life.

MÉNARD ROLLED his eyes in despair when Francine Dion informed him that she had not managed to convince her nephew to let Laura Labelle go. She apologized. Ménard hid his frustration and told her he wanted to know more about Jimmy and his brother.

"Do you think your nephew could hurt his hostage?"

"No, he's a lovely boy. He's been through a lot in his life, you know? Several family members died—my sister, my niece, one of my nephews."

"He never had any problems with the police?"

"God, no. He's the sweetest boy on earth. He wouldn't hurt a fly. He's not socially skilled, that's true. He's a marginal boy. He doesn't have many friends, maybe one or two. He often visits me to keep me company. I'm very sick, you know? If I die, I don't know who's going to take care of him."

"What about Dominic?" Ménard asked.

"Excuse me?"

"Dominic, his brother. He's in the restaurant with him. We're talking to him. From what Jimmy's friend told me, they live together. What can you tell me about him?"

"I don't understand," Francine Dion replied after a few seconds of silence.

Ménard started to get angry. His question had been quite simple. "Mrs. Dion, tell me about your nephew Dominic. He seems very aggressive to me. To be perfectly honest, ma'am, we're not as worried about Jimmy as we are about Dominic."

"But... that's impossible."

"What is impossible?"

"That Dominic is there."

"Why not?"

Francine Dion swallowed hardly.

"Dominic died twenty years ago."

9

Laura had noticed from the very first minutes of the ordeal that Jimmy had issues and that he was in a disturbed state of mind. He was talking to himself, gesturing wildly, as if he was talking to someone else. Like he was talking to a ghost. She played along until she figured out exactly what was going on. She acted as if Dominic existed, as if he were a separate entity. She acknowledged him.

At the same time, she was horrified to watch Jimmy morph into Dominic. The veins in his neck and on his forehead would become prominent. His eyes turned demonic, and his voice deepened, becoming more authoritative than it was when he was Jimmy. While the latter stumbled over his words when he spoke, Dominic spoke fluently and articulately.

But when Jimmy regained control, his face softened, and his eyes became gentle again.

Laura did everything in her power to prevent Dominic from reappearing. She didn't know what triggered his emergence, but she understood that he would take over if she upset Jimmy.

"Who was that person on the phone?" she asked.

"Mind your own business," shouted Dominic.

Laura kept quiet. The call had hurt Jimmy, and Dominic was blocking his feelings, protecting Jimmy by denying him the opportunity to answer Laura's question.

Laura assumed the call had been from someone close to Jimmy. Maybe his mother. Someone who knew his alter ego, because Jimmy had mentioned Dominic as if the person on the call knew him.

The phone rang again, and Jimmy's jaw clenched. He stretched out his arm into the air for Dominic to take the device back. He stood up and turned around to face the chair in which he was sitting, and Laura saw the veins of his neck bulging out before he spoke.

"I said I'd call you. No, you can't talk to him. Jimmy won't speak to anyone. I'm in charge here. Excuse me? Fuck you, man. Fuck you."

Dominic hung up.

"What did he say?" Jimmy asked.

"Nothing. He was trying to convince me that it was you on the phone, that I couldn't be in here. What a bunch of nonsense."

Dominic plunged his dark gaze into Laura's eyes. "If it were up to me, you'd already be dead."

Laura stared at him so intensely that Dominic jumped forward and planted the barrel of his gun against her forehead.

"Look down, you dirty whore. Don't ever look me in the eye again."

She screamed. "Jimmy, please do something! Jimmy, please."

Dominic cocked the hammer of the gun.

"Stop it, Dominic, leave her alone."

"It's all because of her—can't you see it?"

"Dominic, drop the gun right now. This is my fight, not yours."

Dominic lowered his gun. Laura saw Jimmy's features soften.

"So this is your fight, is it?" Dominic said. "Then deal with it." He dropped the gun on the empty chair behind him. Laura had the urge to grab it, but Jimmy quickly picked it up and put it between his belt and his back. He looked at Laura in a way that was meant to be comforting.

Laura let the dust settle a little before she spoke again in a soft voice.

PAUL MÉNARD WANTED Jimmy's aunt to come over and try to reason with him, but she was not well enough to walk. The hostage-taking rumour began to spread on social media, and a few TV vans had already arrived and parked nearby. Ménard dispatched several officers to keep them away. The situation was explosive enough as it was.

Jimmy hadn't answered his phone since Ménard had told him he knew about Dominic. It wasn't the first time Ménard had seen someone with multiple personalities during his career, but this case was the most severe he had ever seen. Being able to switch from one to the other, discussing back and forth like this, was something he had never seen before.

He attempted to reach Laura's phone as well, but again, there was no answer. Her agent told him that she usually kept her phone in her purse. She hadn't had it with her when she was kneeling beside Bruno when they left.

Tougas wondered who had leaked the news of the hostage crisis; the story had spread quickly on social media. He took a look at Mathieu, who was busy with his phone; yes, that was an option. Or maybe it was the deranged man's aunt, or maybe it was the psychopath himself, trying to draw attention to himself. Tougas didn't think it was Bruno; his mind had been elsewhere, dealing with the injury to his foot.

Anyway, it didn't matter anymore. The majority of the messages were sympathetic to Laura's cause, except for a handful of dumbasses who claimed that she had brought the whole thing on herself because of what she had done to François Béliveau. These imbeciles had the audacity to put the hashtag #karma at the end of their ill-advised posts. Tougas restrained himself from insulting them back; he had to stay focused. The priority was to save Laura first.

A journalist he knew well waved at him from a distance, and Tougas walked over and told him that he had no comments at the moment.

"Can you confirm that Laura Labelle is indeed the hostage?"

Tougas hesitated for a few seconds, but there was no point in lying. "Yes, it is her."

"Who's holding her hostage? What does he want?"

"He's obviously a lunatic. I don't know what he wants."

"Tell us how it came down to this."

Other journalists gathered behind the first journalist and pointed their microphones at the agent.

Tougas had said enough. "For now, our priority is Laura's well-being. I will not make any further comments until the situation is resolved, hopefully in a satisfactory manner for everyone. Thank you all for respecting that."

He left, ignoring the cacophony of questions they shouted at him, and walked back to Ménard, who gave him a disapproving glance. Tougas smiled nervously and looked up at the restaurant, crossing his arms.

LAURA HAD TO RELAX. She was afraid of the young man, especially when he switched to his other personality. She knew she had to find a way to keep Jimmy around as long as possible. If she were killed, it would be by the hand of his alter ego, Dominic. Her only hope of salvation was Jimmy.

"They're probably calling your parents right now," she said gently.

Jimmy emerged from his thoughts. "My parents are dead."

So they had something in common. Laura seized the opportunity to use this common point to soften him up. "I'm sorry," she said, looking sad. "My father passed away too."

Jimmy smiled timidly.

"We don't care about your shitty stories," Dominic said, a second after Jimmy smiled. "Jimmy killed our parents and sister, and if he has a shred of sense, he'll kill you too."

Jimmy's face softened, and then he frowned. "What are you talking about? I didn't kill anyone."

"Stop lying to yourself. You know what I'm talking about."

Despite her fears, Laura was fascinated by their dynamics: it was like an actor reciting from a script and responding back to himself, acting as his counterpart.

"Perhaps I can decide," Laura said.

"What do you mean?" Jimmy asked.

"Tell me how your parents died, and I will be happy to share my opinion as to whether or not I believe you are responsible."

"We couldn't care less about your pretentious, petit-bourgeois opinion," Dominic yelled.

"Okay, Dominic," Laura said calmly. "I see you don't want to talk to me about it; I understand that. How about you, Jimmy?"

Jimmy looked at his brother, at least in the direction where he was seeing Dominic, and after a few seconds, he began to tell Laura what had happened to Lydia.

What Jimmy was portraying was the opposite of what she had thought of him from the beginning. Who would have thought that this man, with these undeniable psychological problems, could also be a protective and courageous brother?

"If what you're telling me is correct, you're not responsible for her death, Jimmy. You did everything you could to save her."

Jimmy started laughing unkindly. Laura understood that this was more likely Dominic responding.

She was surprised by her acting skills under the current conditions. She was apparently coming across as a compassionate friend, when all she was trying to accomplish was to find a way to escape. Jimmy couldn't figure that out; she was confident about it.

"So, what do you think he should have done differently, Dominic?" Laura asked. Jimmy's features had become severe.

"Take the high road, get upstairs, kill that motherfucker and bring our sister back willingly or by force. That's what a real man would have done. Jimmy's a coward. He always will be."

"On the contrary," Laura said, "I know a few people who would have dared to confront the pimp alone, without any police help."

"I would have killed him like a goddamn dog in an alley, and Lydia would be alive today," Dominic answered in a resentful tone.

"Easy to say when you're not there. You're like an armchair quarterback, questioning judgments after the fact." Laura closed her eyes. She had said it more aggressively than she would have liked.

Dominic sprang up in front of her, foaming at the mouth, screaming, his face a few centimetres from hers. He had the gun barrel under her chin now.

She opened her eyes and looked into Dominic's. His glance was so evil that she felt a shiver of fear go down her spine.

"I told you not to look at me. I'm going to kill you like a whore."

Laura closed her eyes, wishing the storm would end. For

several more high-intensity minutes, Dominic kept shouting at her, his spittle spraying her face, his face reddened with rage. She whispered Jimmy's name a few times, loud enough for him to hear it.

"Jimmy, help me. Jimmy, please."

No reaction.

She laid her hand gently on his arm. "Jimmy, help me. He's going to kill me."

The screaming stopped abruptly, and as she slowly opened her eyes, she recognized Jimmy's relaxed features. Dominic had left. Jimmy stared at Laura's hand on his arm.

"Dom, calm down. She's right; you weren't there. Killing her pimp wouldn't have helped. If Lydia had wanted me to rescue her, she could have followed me instead of running away from me like she did. I did everything I could to help her, but she was running away from me."

Jimmy stared at the floor as if he was trying to persuade himself. Laura sensed that he was feeling guilty, but when he reflected out loud, he clearly recognized the situation as it was and found some solace in it.

The phone rang. Jimmy pulled himself together and handed the phone over again.

"Maybe you should do the talking, Jimmy," Laura said.

"She's playing us against each other, Jimmy. Can't you see it?"

Jimmy was still holding the phone up in the air. He didn't answer.

"Look, if I can tell them I'm not hurt, maybe they'll give you a break," Laura explained.

Jimmy looked at the actress for a few seconds before handing her the phone.

"Hello?"

Ménard was surprised to hear a female voice on the phone. His heart pounded. "Laura?"

Tougas rushed to the officer upon hearing his client's name.

"Yes, this is me."

"I'm Paul Ménard, from the Montréal Police Department. Are you all right?"

"Yes, I'm fine."

"You're not hurt, are you?"

"No, I'm okay," Laura replied, looking at Jimmy as he grinned with a contrite look.

Ménard signalled to Tougas that everything was fine. Tougas tilted his head backwards and sighed with relief.

"Is Jimmy still with you?"

"Yes, Jimmy and Dominic are here."

Laura didn't know why she'd said that, but she hoped that by acknowledging Dominic's presence, she would get a little sympathy from him.

"Laura, we know that Dominic and Jimmy are the same person. I suggest you don't encourage his fantasies."

"I disagree with your suggestion."

Jimmy looked at Laura with a frown. Laura waved at him, signalling him not to worry.

"Laura, listen to me, I'm a hostage-taking specialist. You have to trust me. Dominic is Jimmy's twin brother. He died when they were six years old. You have to find a way to get Jimmy to understand that his brother is the product of his imagination. Because if I understand correctly, Dominic is the one who is dangerous, right?"

"Indeed."

"So, subtly, try to make him realize that his brother is dead and that he's in control of his fate. His aunt told us he wouldn't hurt anybody. That he's a good guy."

Paul Ménard quickly described the details of Dominic's death, as told by Jimmy's aunt. He knew he had to be quick: the situation had been stagnant for too long, proof that Dominic was leading the way. As long as it was like that, Laura was in great danger.

Laura realized she had to figure out how to confront Jimmy with his imaginary brother.

Jimmy waved at her to hand him the phone back.

"I have to say goodbye now. Please tell my agent that the eagle has landed. Thank you."

"The eagle what? Laura?"

Jimmy grabbed the phone and stood up.

"You talked to her, Ménard. Now leave us alone."

"Jimmy?"

"No, this is Dominic. I've told you a thousand times that I am in charge of communications."

"Listen to me, Jimmy," Ménard said. "You haven't done anything serious yet. You're still—"

"I. AM. DOMINIC!" he screamed before hanging up.

Ménard hung up the phone, furious.

"Is she wounded?"

Tougas looked utterly overwhelmed. It's normal, Ménard thought. Who wouldn't be?

"She's shaken up, but she's not upset. She told me she wasn't hurt."

"Is that all?"

"Yes. Actually, no. She told me to tell you something I didn't grasp. Something about an eagle doing something."

The agent's face became brighter. "The eagle has landed?"

"Yes, that's right. The eagle has landed. You look relieved; what does that mean?"

"It's an inside joke between the actors of the show. When someone masters his lines, he tells others that the eagle has landed. What I understand from this is that she is in enough control of the situation to reassure us."

Ménard had difficulty understanding the metaphor but shrugged it off. It was irrelevant at this stage. Still, it reassured him that the hostage was not panicking. He hoped that she would follow his advice. Jimmy had to be taken out of his stupor. Ménard didn't know him, but what he had heard about Dominic didn't comfort him.

Not at all.

10

L aura was surprised by the emotion she felt when she shared the story of her father's death with Jimmy. She didn't have to act this time. As time went on, she relaxed more whenever Jimmy was around. Things became worse when Dominic was involved, but it had been a while since he had shown any signs of life. Was it because her strategy was effective?

Jimmy had been sitting comfortably for a while before Laura mentioned that he still hadn't talked about his own parents' deaths. He stiffened up and said that his father had died in a car accident.

"Did your brother die in the same accident as your father?"

She might as well take a shot at it, she thought. See how Jimmy was going to react.

He stared at her, confused. "Are you talking about my sister's death?"

Laura was searching for the right words.

"Don't you have a brother who passed away?"

"No."

Laura was too nervous to tell him that Dominic was dead, as Ménard had recommended; she didn't want him to reappear.

"My mistake. I thought you had a brother who died when you were six."

Jimmy shook his head without conviction. No sign of Dominic.

She went on. "What about your mother?"

Jimmy's eyes darkened to such an extent that Laura feared she had gone too far. But Jimmy opened up after a moment of reflection as if he wanted to tell the story correctly.

His mother had been depressed for years, he began. She had never recovered from her husband's death. Jimmy had tried so hard to cheer her up, but there was nothing he could do. She refused to see a psychiatrist, insisting that she was not crazy. After several unsuccessful attempts, he decided to change his strategy and left her alone, acting as if nothing had happened. Perhaps she only needed to be by herself for a while. Jimmy distracted her the best he could, but nothing seemed to work.

One day when he came home from school, he found his mother cutting her wrists. He jumped on her, tore the knife out of her hands and pinned her to the floor until she stopped screaming at him to let her die. Finally, she calmed down, but Jimmy had had enough. He picked up the phone to call the hospital and ask them to come and pick up his mother. She needed care.

She begged him to hang up, not to do that to her. She loathed hospitals. She wasn't crazy; she had only had a moment of sadness. She promised him that it would never happen again. Jimmy looked down at his mother kneeling, wrapping her arms around his legs, imploring him not to do this to her. He felt sorry for her.

He hung up the phone.

He trusted her.

The next morning, he found her hanging from a fixture in the bedroom ceiling. Sobbing, he cut her down and held her body in his arms, screaming in despair. He laid her on her bed, loosened the sheets tied around her neck and covered her with the same sheets before kissing her on the forehead. That day, he swore that he would never let anyone else he loved die. No one he cared about would ever again suffer the same fate. He had succeeded, until Lydia died.

Jimmy finished speaking and sat quietly, looking at the floor. Laura cried in silence. She could not conceive that a human being could experience so much pain in such a short time. It was enough to drive anyone crazy. Surprisingly, she wanted to hug and console him, probably because of her maternal instincts. Maybe her mother was right; she was too kind. She always saw good in others. She couldn't help it.

All Jimmy needed was to be loved and, of course, to get psychiatric care.

She vowed to do everything in her power to help him. If she made it out alive.

To that end, she decided she would pretend to have Stockholm syndrome and feign sympathy with Jimmy's cause. She had heard about this phenomenon while studying for a role at the acting school. It was a psychological reaction that sometimes occurred in hostages who had been close to their abductors for an extended period of time. In the early 1970s, a jail-breaker had attempted to rob a bank in Sweden but failed. At first, the ten frightened employees had been justifiably terrified of him, but they had ended up feeling sympathy for their captor and developing resentment against the police. Some of them had even acted as human shields to protect him. Laura had been fascinated by the story, even if she couldn't understand how anybody could side with someone who had set out to harm them.

Although she wanted to get out of this situation and had no

hard feelings towards the police, Laura also could not deny that she had developed sympathy for Jimmy. Apart from getting out of this ordeal alive, her goal was to find a way for Jimmy to get the care he needed and get rid of his brother's ghost, to live a healthy life.

But first, she had to take care of Dominic. A renewed will had given her the strength to go for it, to take Paul Ménard's advice and gamble that Jimmy could overcome Dominic.

"When you say you did everything you could for your mother," Laura said, "you mean Lydia, Dominic and you?"

Jimmy reflected for a moment. "You're right about Lydia. Dom was no longer in contact with us at that time."

"Where was he?"

Jimmy shrugged.

"With your father?"

"No, my father was already deceased, remember?"

Laura saw a breach. "How long did you lose contact with Dominic?"

"For a couple of years."

Laura was expecting Dominic's sudden return any second now. "How old were you when you lost contact?"

"I was a child. I would say about six or eight years old."

Laura's heart was pounding faster. "And when did you reconnect?"

"A little after Lydia's death."

Laura remained silent. She was anxious to find out the right way to wake up Jimmy's memory about his brother's death, but she had to find a way to keep Dominic on the sidelines. She suspected that Jimmy had made up Dominic's return to compensate for Lydia's death. Without him, Jimmy was alone in the world.

Laura thought wistfully about Jimmy's sweet, sad eyes. She wondered what would have been the outcome for him if he hadn't had so many tragedies in his life. If life hadn't punched him so many times right in the heart.

In an effort not to get too sentimental, Laura reminded herself of Bruno's pain, caused by Jimmy and his gun. She needed to keep in mind that Jimmy wasn't sane and not allow her feelings to take over. First things first. She'd be pleading in favour of Jimmy at the tribunal, but for now, all that mattered was getting out of there.

Suddenly, Jimmy began to applaud slowly, a sarcastic look on his face.

Damn it.

Dominic.

11

The angry looks, the crazy stare, the clenched jaw. All the evil in the world in the facial features.

No doubt, Dominic was back.

"I must admit, I underestimated you, my dear. Jimmy's going to believe that you have empathy for him. But you don't fool me. You're an actress. You're acting. You may be deceiving him, but you're not deceiving me."

"Where is Jimmy?" she asked, alarmed.

"As you can see, he went for a walk—too much emotion for him, poor thing. Getting him to talk about his mother, father and sister—I have to confess, it was ingenious. But you and I both know you don't care."

Laura felt chills all over her body.

Dominic got up and, with a theatrical gesture, mimicked shaking a Magic 8-Ball. "Tell me, Magic 8-Ball, what are the odds of Laura getting out of here alive?" His tone was mocking and vicious. Pretending to read, he looked at Laura with a fake pout of disappointment. "Slim to none."

"Where were you, Dominic?"

He looked at her, not understanding what she was talking about.

"During all those years, when you had little contact with Jimmy and Lydia, where were you?"

"It's none of your business."

"The truth is, you don't know, right?"

"Shut the fuck up."

Dominic's jaws tightened. He looked like he was about to explode into rage like a wild animal, but at that point, Laura had nothing more to lose. She had to go all-in.

"Dominic, do you recall the car accident with your father?"

"I said shut up, you stupid bitch."

"Do you remember the sound of twisted metal when the van hit your car?"

"You fucking bitch. I will silence you."

"Do you remember your father after the crash? Did he die instantly? Did you suffer?"

"I'm going to kill you!"

Dominic jumped out of his chair and lunged for Laura's throat with both hands. She fell backwards, hitting her head hard on the floor. She could feel Dominic's powerful fingers crushing her neck. Soon, her eyesight faded due to the impact of her head on the floor and the air that was cruelly lacking. She managed to whisper, "Jimmy... Jimmy..."

But Jimmy didn't step in.

Laura's body was weakening by the seconds. The light from the restaurant was fading. The darkness filled her eyes, and she let go. She gently touched Jimmy's face one last time before sinking into obscurity.

PAUL MÉNARD INSTRUCTED the snipers to aim at the restaurant's main window and the SWAT team to position themselves with their shields near the front door, along the brick wall on the left.

The screams coming from the interior told him, beyond doubt, that it was time for the police to break in. The actress's life was in danger; every second counted.

Ménard told one of the officers to take Mike Tougas and his wife away from the building. Laura Labelle's mother, who had arrived a few minutes earlier, was standing further away with other police officers on the other side of the security perimeter. She was crying, imploring Laura's father to help them.

No more noise was coming from the restaurant; no more fighting, no more yelling. There were no shots fired.

Then the yelling resumed as if two men were fighting. Had he not known that Jimmy was alone inside, Ménard would have thought there were two of them. There was a bright, high-pitched voice he attributed to Jimmy and a dark, grave voice, similar to Dominic's on the phone.

Ménard looked up to make sure that the two snipers were in position; they were perched on the roof of a building across the street from the restaurant. In front of him, four SWAT agents were waiting for his signal to break down the door and throw blinding grenades.

Paul Ménard raised his arm and brought his walkie-talkie to his mouth.

"Wait for my signal."

~

DOMINIC WAS KNEELING next to Laura Labelle's inert body. He had killed her. He felt no remorse. It was unavoidable. She had humiliated her brother. She deserved to die.

"What have you done, for the love of God?" Jimmy said, screaming.

"What you should have done a long time ago," Dominic replied.

"She was playing you, and you were too stupid to see it."

Dominic felt the muzzle of the gun against his head.

"I'm going to kill you, you motherfucker. You killed the woman of my dreams. I'm going to kill you, you monster."

Dominic laughed. "You are indeed good at murdering family members, Jimmy. Are you going to do the same with me? Then shoot."

"You are done lying to me, Dominic. I've been through enough of your lies. All those years, you made me feel guilty about Lydia and Mom's death."

"Oh, poor Jimmy. Don't you know that you can only feel guilty when you have something to blame yourself for?"

Jimmy didn't answer. Dominic continued.

"I mean, if you haven't done anything, no one can make you carry the blame. You know very well that you let them both die. And now you have to live with the death of your beloved actress. Everything you touch turns to shit, Jimmy."

"Fuck you," Jimmy said, cocking the hammer of the gun.

Dominic panicked. "Whoa, whoa, Jimmy. Think before you act. She deserved to die; didn't you see how she humiliated you this afternoon? How she failed to defend you when the security guard took you out and shamed you before handing you over to the two female police officers?"

Jimmy froze. "How do you know that?"

"How do I know what?" Dominic replied angrily.

"About the two women cops."

"You told me that."

"No, I never told you that. I told you I was in the custody of the police. I know I didn't tell you the truth because I didn't want you to make fun of me. If I'd said two female police officers escorted me, you would have made fun of me. I knew you'd blame me for not breaking out of their grip and returning to the mall."

Dominic didn't answer. He rolled his eyes and sighed. "You told me, Jimmy. Otherwise, how else would I know? Stop screwing around."

"The only way you would know that without me telling you is if you had been there."

"You know very well that I wasn't there, because it would have gone much differently than it did, believe me."

Jimmy carried on. "I know you weren't there. You're never there for me. And I know I didn't tell you about the two cops."

"You're losing your mind. I'm always here for you."

Jimmy turned back to Laura and looked at her as his eyes filled with tears. She was dead because of him; this time, it was true. He could blame Dominic for whatever he wanted, but it was he who had pulled out his gun; it was he who had shot the man in the foot. It was he who had listened to Dominic and taken her hostage. And now she was dead.

Jimmy squatted down and caressed Laura's face as tears ran down his cheeks. "I'm sorry, Laura, I'm so sorry."

"Fucking hell, what a loser," Dominic said in the background, laughing.

Jimmy stopped stroking the actress's face but remained crouched down, closing his eyes, his back turned to his brother.

"Where were you, Dominic? All this time, where have you been?"

"Don't start with that too, for heaven's sake."

Jimmy got up and turned to his brother. "You never answered Laura's question. Where have you been all this time?"

Dominic rolled his eyes. "Stop messing around. You know very well where I was."

"As a matter of fact, I don't. What about the car accident she was referring to?"

"See, she made all that up, Jimmy. Don't be ridiculous."

Jimmy walked up to his brother and pointed his gun at him. "Don't lie to me," he shouted. "Be honest for once in your fucking life."

"Wow," said Dominic as he held his hand to his heart. "That one hurts. It hurts like hell. I'm not going to lie." He smirked.

Jimmy cocked the gun and pointed it at Dominic's face.

"Tell me the truth about the accident!"

Dominic threw his arms up in the air. "Okay, okay, okay. Holy shit. Fuck. You can be stubborn when you want. Yes, that's right. I was with Dad in the accident. He died instantly. That's what you wanted to hear?"

Jimmy looked at him with fear. He had just realized something. Something that had been hidden all this time but that had suddenly become crystal clear.

"What's the matter? You look weird," Dominic said, losing some of his arrogance.

"I don't remember seeing you after Dad died. Why can't I remember you being with us before you came back after Lydia's death? I'll ask you one more time: where were you?"

Dominic quietly lowered his arms as he looked at his brother with softness for the first time in a long time. He shrugged. "What do you want me to say, Jimmy?"

"Tell me where the fuck you were."

Jimmy looked at his brother with tremendous sorrow in his eyes. Dominic quietly backed away, sat down in a chair and looked at the floor.

"Dominic?"

After a few seconds, Jimmy repeated his question. Dominic looked straight at him. "I don't know."

"You don't know what?" Jimmy's heart was beating fast. His head was spinning.

"I don't know where I was."

Jimmy sat down as well. Nothing made sense anymore. How could someone have no idea where they'd been for years?

It didn't make any sense. Then suddenly it was as though a light bulb had flicked on. He realized what was happening. Immediately, he felt his heart break in two. All this time—was it possible?

"What are you going to do, Jimmy? What are you thinking about?"

Jimmy turned the gun around in his hand so the grip would face forward, and with a quick and powerful gesture, crushed it in the middle of his forehead.

Jimmy bent over in pain as he dropped the gun at his feet. For a moment, he thought he was going to lose consciousness, but he held out until the pain was sustainable. He felt a hot, thick fluid dripping onto his hand, which rested on his forehead. He didn't need to check what it was; it was his blood.

Jimmy looked up at his brother, who was staring back at him with a dazed look. Dominic remained silent. He knew what was happening.

Jimmy merely looked at the massive wound in his brother's forehead, identical to the one he had just inflicted on himself; the blood was flowing profusely. Jimmy had hoped he was wrong. But no: he had to face the facts. Dominic only existed in his head. All this time, Dominic hadn't been there at all. Everything made sense now: Dominic's reluctance to do things with him, his homebody temperament, his inability to find a job. His lack of a love life. Jimmy understood why all Dominic did was meddle with his life, advise him, denigrate him.

Dominic was Jimmy's self-destructive conscience.

He, Jimmy, was the one who had killed Laura, not Dominic.

He fell to his knees. He was insane. Anyone who had ever laughed at him and told him he wasn't normal had been right.

He heard a moan behind him and saw Laura's feet moving.

"Laura, you're alive!"

Laura quietly adjusted her eyes as she rubbed her throat.

She had trouble talking and swallowing. Why did Jimmy have a bloody face?

"Laura, I know about Dominic. I'm going to get you out of here. I'm going to turn myself in. I'm going to get treatment. You're all I have left in the world, even though I know it's not mutual. Even though I know you hate me."

Laura remained mute.

"Finish her," Dominic shouted.

How was it possible he was still there? Jimmy knew that Dominic didn't really exist, so why was he standing right there in front of him?

"Give me the gun if you're not up for it," Dominic ordered.

Jimmy spotted the gun on the ground to his right. He kicked the weapon hard, and it slid under a table.

"Asshole," Dominic said to him as he ran towards the gun.

Jimmy bent over to help Laura get up.

"Come quickly."

She could barely move; there was a terrible pain in her head. Jimmy dragged her to the other end of the restaurant, in front of a large window covered by thick curtains.

He sat Laura on a chair and looked behind him. Dominic had the gun in his hand and was heading towards them. Jimmy spotted the keys on the counter behind his brother and his heart began to beat faster. He had to find a way to get Laura out quickly before Dominic caught up with them.

Jimmy quickly pulled the curtains aside and was blinded by the spotlights of the SWAT trucks. He grabbed a chair to his left and threw it through the window, which burst into a thousand pieces. He then helped Laura through the gap and out of the restaurant. Once she was out, Jimmy was about to surrender and raise his arms when he saw a man holding up his left arm; he was wearing a bulletproof jacket with the word POLICE on it. Jimmy looked down and saw that he had the Glock in his right hand.

As soon as Jimmy's eyes met the officer's, the man vigorously lowered his arm.

Two deafening noises, like firecrackers, broke out in the night. Jimmy was thrown backward and spun around. He collapsed face down onto the restaurant floor; the revolver flew out of his hand and slid away. He attempted to get up but fell back down again.

He heard muffled voices of men shouting and saw human-shaped shadows approaching. Turning his head to the side, he saw Laura approaching and looking at him from the outside, a hand covering her mouth.

Quickly, she was escorted away by a man in a SWAT uniform. Jimmy saw no sign of fear or hate in her eyes. Instead, he saw only worry, as if she wanted to see whether he was alive.

Jimmy had succeeded. Laura was safe. Not only had he not killed her, but he had saved her from Dominic.

He had saved her from himself.

Hot liquid filled his throat and leaked out of his mouth. He had trouble breathing; it felt as if someone was pressing so hard against his chest that his rib cage would implode.

He turned his head to the other side to see where Dominic was, but he couldn't find him.

Just as he was about to faint, a shape moved towards him. A child's feet stopped a few centimetres from his face. A small silhouette leaned towards him, and he recognized young Dominic's face, the same as in his memories. His little brother smiled at him as he watched him with affection. Dominic reached out to him, but Jimmy was unable to move.

"Come on, try harder," said his brother's little voice.

Jimmy drew on his last resources and struggled to get up. Then he was standing, holding Dominic's little hand in his own. Standing in front of them was Lydia, wearing a radiant smile, and a little further on, their mother and father, almost like two holograms.

Jimmy knew at that moment that he would never be alone again.

He looked down behind him and saw his dislocated body, pierced with bullets, beside which two men in SWAT uniforms were working to resuscitate him.

They would not succeed.

There was no way Jimmy was going back there.

He looked around and saw bystanders trying to see what was going on. He spotted Laura crying in a woman's arms. Probably her mother. Then, as he was about to leave, Laura turned her head, and her eyes met Jimmy's. At least, that's what he thought. And then, even though he knew it was impossible, he thought he saw her smiling through the tears.

"Let's go," Dominic said.

His little brother dragged him towards the rest of his family, who had already started to walk away. He didn't know where they were going, and he didn't care.

He was with his family. That was all that mattered.

fter a few days, Laura was discharged from the hospital. She was resting at home with Bruno, who also needed to recover. Several bones in his foot had been shattered, but the doctors had told him that he would eventually walk normally again. The surgeons had installed metal plates to weld the remaining bones of his foot together.

Laura had asked her family not to discuss what had happened. At least, for the upcoming weeks, until this was settled. She was still upset about the nightmare she'd experienced, and was taking sleeping pills. She kept to herself that often at night, she woke up in a sweat. She would see Dominic's crazy eyes staring at her again; she would try to scream, but no sound would come out. In the dreams, she would try to distinguish Jimmy from Dominic, even though they shared the same body.

On other occasions, she would think about Jimmy's soft, warm face, and she would not feel any fear. But then, she would see flashbacks of Jimmy spinning in the air, swirling around, hear the monstrous sound of the two shots and see his body crashing loudly to the floor.

She couldn't help but see a connection with her father's death. Sometimes she wondered if there was any subtle meaning to all of this. Why had she witnessed two men dying in front of her and crashing face-first to the ground? She would probably never have an answer to that question; perhaps it was just a coincidence. At least that was the conclusion she had reached.

She had mixed feelings about what happened. On the one hand, she was grateful to the police for having done everything in their power to save her life, but at the same time, she felt that they had been quick to pull the trigger.

Jimmy had deserved a chance, she thought, to be taken care of, to get treatment. He could have started a new life and finally been happy.

He hadn't deserved to die.

When she was in her mother's arms that night, shortly after Jimmy had helped her escape, she had looked back inside the restaurant as two men were trying to resuscitate him. She had suddenly had a premonition that Jimmy would be okay. No matter where he was, Laura felt in her soul that Jimmy would be safe. Call it a hunch or whatever, but when she'd left that night, she had no longer been worried about him.

It was a bizarre feeling.

People said he was a maniac, that he didn't deserve her affection for him, but how would they know? She often thought about what had happened, but she knew that time would make things better. It was always like that. One day, life would resume, and all this would be a distant memory.

For now, it made her angry to read what people said about Jimmy. All the nicknames they gave to him. The video of Jimmy being kicked out of the signing session had gone viral. She had only watched it once, but she felt sorry for him. Jimmy, and not Dominic, was the one on that video, with the desperate look on his face, screaming her name.

She wondered how things would have turned out if she had agreed to talk to him; if she had reassured him that no one wanted to kill her. That everything was fine. Would it have ended with a signed poster and a photograph like all the others? That's what she liked to think.

Initially, she had thought Jimmy had just been clumsy in his approach. But then, she'd realized there was no right way to do what he wanted to do. He had had no chance to succeed.

She had also stumbled upon a video of François Béliveau with his new squeeze and heard the derogatory comments he made about her. She didn't know why, but somehow, she wondered how Jimmy would have reacted if he had read that.

He would have been furious.

Laura thought it was sad that a fundamentally good man like Jimmy was the target of cruel taunts by people who didn't know him. And that a jerk like François Béliveau was worshipped by these same assholes who didn't know him any better.

It was all about image. It was a shame.

"Are you lost in thought, darling?"

She smiled at Bruno, who had just come back, limping, with two lattes.

Laura had been angry for a few days at Bruno for initiating the confrontation with Jimmy. If he had just gone out of the restaurant as he was supposed to, she was sure that Jimmy wouldn't have done anything. His friend Mathieu, the waiter that night, had confirmed that Jimmy had dropped the idea of telling her about his suspicions regarding the producers of the show. He didn't want to have to relive the humiliation he had experienced in the shopping mall earlier that day. Mathieu admitted that he had called Jimmy that night to tell him that Laura was at the restaurant. He'd thought Jimmy just wanted to make sure she was safe and observe her from a distance, as he usually did.

Mathieu had apologized several times to Laura about this. She told him that he had nothing to be sorry about.

The only question she had yet to answer was why Jimmy had brought a gun with him to the restaurant. No one knew for sure, but Laura was convinced that Dominic had compelled him to take it with him. Or maybe he had taken it along for protection in case someone recognized him from the mall and wanted to hurt him.

She eventually forgave Bruno. She knew he meant well. He had overreacted, but the intention was right. He had also apologized so often that Laura made him swear not to talk about it anymore. She no longer wanted them to focus on this dark moment in their lives.

They had to look forward. So, they concluded that overcoming this ordeal would make them stronger.

As she took a sip of her excellent hot coffee, she smiled at Bruno and told him that he could start the film they were about to see on Netflix. She leaned her head on her boyfriend's shoulder, delighted to realize that she loved him as much as ever.

She wondered if, one day, she would be rid of the latent sadness that had been inhabiting her since that day.

She hoped so, even though she knew she would be linked to Jimmy for life.

For better or for worse.

YOU CAN MAKE A DIFFERENCE

The reviews you leave represent the most formidable weapons in my arsenal in terms of the visibility for my books. As an independent author, I don't have the marketing resources offered by the major publishing houses. I can't buy a full page of a major daily newspaper or TV commercials. That is correct, that is my choice and I fully accept it.

However, I have something more powerful. Something those big publishing houses would kill for.

You, my readers.

Your honest opinion of my books helps to attract the attention of other readers who do not know me.

So if you enjoyed this book, I would be extremely grateful if you would take a few minutes to leave your opinion on the website from where you bought this book.

Thank you again for your help. It is very much appreciated.

LET'S STAY IN CONTACT

One of the most important things in my writing career is to build a strong relationship with my readers. Without you, none of this would be possible.

You're the reason I write.

I have a lot of stories in mind and not just in the Martin Lafs series. I have other worlds to show you, and I very much hope that you will be part of that journey with me.

I invite you to subscribe to my monthly newsletter. My goal is to create exciting content for you, and I will adjust it according to your comments.

In addition to news about new releases and exclusive promotions only for my newsletter subscribers, I will share my top suggestions for the months on several topics.

I will describe my travels around the world, my life as an author, what genuinely happens behind the stage, news about me, etc.

Also, you can download the Martin Lafs prequel for free by joining the mailing list. It can only be found this way. It's not available on any store.

To register, go on my website (https://sebastyendugas.com)
Thank you again for your interest.

ABOUT THE AUTHOR

Sebastyen Dugas is a French-Canadian author from Montreal, Quebec, Canada. He publishes in both French and English. He holds a bachelor's degree in business administration and has worked in IT for most of his career.

Always having had a love of the written word, Sebastyen has been writing since he was young, penning articles for blogs and as a journalist for multiple publications. He had never come close to publishing, as he was content to do it for his own enjoyment, but all that has now changed with his first novel, now released on an unsuspecting world. Impatient by nature, he decided to go as an independent author instead of going the traditional route.

In his spare time Sebastyen loves reading, playing guitar, photography, most sports and watching movies. He is also slowly working his way around the countries of the world, having now visited 20 of them and exploring some amazing places and sights as he goes along with his girlfriend.

In the future he hopes to continue with his wide and varied travels, write more fiction and enjoy life to the full.

You can contact, follow or just see what Sebastyen Dugas by following him on these different platform.

facebook.com/sebastyendugaswriter

twitter.com/TalkWithTheY

ALSO BY SEBASTYEN DUGAS